I0595210

John Saunders

One Against the World

Vol. 2

John Saunders

One Against the World
Vol. 2

ISBN/EAN: 9783337346607

Printed in Europe, USA, Canada, Australia, Japan

Cover: Foto ©Andreas Hilbeck / pixelio.de

More available books at **www.hansebooks.com**

ONE AGAINST THE WORLD;

OR,

REUBEN'S WAR.

A Novel.

BY

JOHN SAUNDERS,

AUTHOR OF "ABEL DRAKE'S WIFE," "GUY WATERMAN," ETC.

IN THREE VOLUMES.

VOL. II.

LONDON:

TINSLEY BROTHERS, 18, CATHERINE ST., STRAND.

1865.

[*The Right of Translation is reserved.*]

LONDON:
BRADBURY AND EVANS, PRINTERS, WHITEFRIARS.

CONTENTS.

vi   CONTENTS.

ONE AGAINST THE WORLD;

OR,

REUBEN'S WAR.

CHAPTER I.

THE STORY GOES ON ONCE MORE.

SWELL JACK'S appeal to Reuben proved the turning point of our hero's final decision and destiny. He changed colour—muttered faltering words of refusal, which were easily overpowered by the utterances of Swell Jack's bolder policy and skilful suggestion. It was, however, despair with regard to Bella rather than hope of the favour of the lady at St. John's Wood that made the temptation so irresistible. He was yielding— when there was heard a knock, and, to Reuben's astonishment, Bella appeared at the door.

He had not seen her for many days. He had, indeed, at last given up the hope of ever seeing her again, except in some surreptitious sort of way, which he had determined to adopt before he departed. And yet she was now here, coming to his chamber! Nay, coming to it when this showy stranger was present!

If the visit were inexplicable, still more so was the cause of its being made. She merely said :—

"Would you like some refreshment for your friend?" while her face looked pale, and her voice slightly trembled as if with half-suppressed agitation.

Was it possible *she* had come merely to say that? The servant always now came to answer his bell, or to supply his daily wants. Had her mother sent her, or been willing to let her come? All these questions ran rapidly through Reuben's mind, but he was quite unable to answer them.

As to the refreshments, the friend himself said—

"Thank you, I'm hungry, and should be very glad of a crust of bread and cheese and a glass of ale."

Bella bent her head slightly in acknowledg-ment of his speech, and looked in silence towards Reuben, whose glance met her glance, then fell, and she drew the door after her and was gone. She did not come again, as Reuben expected and hoped. The servant brought a tray with cold fowl and wine, as well as with the humbler articles Swell Jack had asked for; but Bella appeared not, nor was any remark made by either of the two men about her. But the moment of her appearance had removed whatever of danger to Reuben existed in the temptation offered to him. All the things so lately said to him seemed to be gone and utterly forgotten. Bella's`image absorbed his whole being.

Had she been conscious of what was going on in that chamber? Or had she simply suspected what sort of man the visitor might be, and what sort of business he came upon, and determined to forget for a moment her repugnance to seeing him again, in the desire to quicken his good resolutions, if indeed they were failing?

It was, for the time, a sweet delusion to Reuben to think it must have been so, even if it could be proved to be a delusion directly after. But was it a delusion? He had got to be almost superstitious as to her influence over him—as to the connection between her love and his regeneration—as to the mingling of their future fates.

When Swell Jack had thoroughly satisfied his appetite, and smoked another cigar through, he began, without saying another word on the subject of Reuben's departure, to collect such things as he saw lying about. But Reuben stopped him at once by saying, in a clear, cold, determined tone of voice,

" Thank you, Jack, all the same, for your kindness, but I have quite made up my mind. I shall go on as I have begun, and win, if I can win, the prize I have in view."

" Very well ; I confess I am sorry, but I'll say no more. Good luck, old fellow, and good-by! If I don't make haste I shan't catch the express train up to-night. Good-by ! "

They shook hands and parted. And as Reuben heard Swell Jack go out at the door, he heard him say to the ladies,

" I wish you both a very good morning, ladies. I have come on a fruitless errand, and I don't mind saying so, or telling you it wasn't one you would approve of. I wanted my friend to go back with me, and he won't. Once more I wish you a very good morning."

And Reuben knew that in saying this Swell Jack had magnanimously forgotten his defeat; and sought, by sacrificing his own character, to give a lift to his friend's, by letting them see that Reuben was resolved not to return to the old life.

After that Reuben was better able to go on with his story.

That last touch of magnanimity on the part of his former friend—the letting himself down from his assumed position of gentleman and honest man in order to raise him (Reuben) up in the estimation of the people of the house, by making them see his determination to keep to the new career he had begun—this unexpected act of chivalry— touched our hero so much that he could not help looking from the window upon the retreating form with a strong desire to call it back, and confess himself conquered. And he probably would have done so, but for his thoughts of Bella —his reverting to the deeply-interesting speculation—had she come intentionally at so critical a moment, guessing how much so it was for him? It was impossible to answer the question. Perhaps it might never be answered. Meantime he could not refuse to believe in it as a token that her heart was still turned towards him.

But the visit had another and peculiar effect. It set Reuben thinking of the many excellent qualities he had seen developed even among thieves, and of the foolish way in which, as it seemed to him, society tries to keep down the dangerous classes. He was no philosopher, but he felt instinctively that there was in these classes a vast fund of available skill and energy which might be of the greatest value to the community, instead of being used as now to prey upon it. Dimly there was hovering through his mind some idea of making his own life the subject of an instructive sketch, by showing the truth. And no doubt it would be of the greatest value if we could obtain from such men accurate records of all their doings, views, and feelings. If our prison chaplains would attend to this when they first come into communication with criminals, how different might be the result! If they would only win the hearts of such men by inducing them frankly to tell their several stories — making them aware that the knowledge should be religiously guarded from injuring them — then, indeed, we might soon see how to make prison reformation a vital and a holy truth. For then we should see the absurdity of treating so many different characters all with the same kind of cast-iron discipline. We should then perceive that the sternness that might be absolutely necessary to influence this man might be cruel and ruinous to that one. We should learn that the professions of one prisoner might be rightly treated as of no value whatever, so long as they were not fortified by long periods of actual well-doing; while the mere promise of another might be the result of a great change, and deserve implicit credit. Yet, to make inquiries of this kind in this spirit is about the last thing that Government officials ever think of. But not the less is this the one question in the life of every felon that *must* be determined before we can cure him, or extinguish the class of criminals to which he belongs by the extinction of its causes—*How did he become what he is?*

There are no apparent limits to the amount of money, skill, and time that we are willing to spend on the consideration or treatment of the symptoms of crime. New model prisons, new theories which have every kind of excellent quality about them except that of being based on a true and profound knowledge of human nature —bulky volumes of prison reports and statistics —long discussions in Parliament—all these things show how serious is the evil we have to grapple with; but also how aimless, and confused, and inefficient are our operations, except for the catching and punishing a certain small per-centage of existing offenders, after they have been allowed to grow up and to flourish as offenders. To repress seems the one and only idea. And when we have for the moment suc-ceeded, and driven the foul eruptions inward, we are amazed and shocked beyond measure at the wickedness of human nature that persists in breaking out elsewhere in the same evil way, but with tenfold force. The quacks of the body are falling into disrepute ; when will the quacks who hang about the mind and character of men share the same fate ?

"I have shown," wrote Reuben as he recommenced, after some long and painful cogitation over these problems, "how I became that which I am. I have not imposed this fearful duty upon myself so much in expiation to society as perhaps I ought to have done. My object has been and is more selfish and personal. But, still, here are the chief facts; and if they can some day be made useful to others, I shall be glad. But ask me not also to describe in detail the life I have gone through. Ask me not to show how I spent, month by month or year by year, the next few years of my career. The pen quivers in my hand, the flesh creeps upon my bones, as my busy recollection, writing in this home of peace and innocence, recalls some of the many scenes of private vice, public exposure, and alternations of bitter suffering and want, with hours and days of riotous indulgence when fortune favoured me (to use my own phrase) with ample means. But there are certain features of my career that I cannot pass over in silence, and chiefly my connection with the man who fell by my hands in this very house.

"Ah! how well I remember the dreadful night on which we first met. My mother was dead and buried, Barrett had been transported, I had been for some weeks my own master, and had spent my time chiefly in helping a neighbour—a maker of cheap musical instruments. But he was, though honest, an inveterate drunkard; and when drunk became alike suspicious and abusive. The very first quarrel we had he told me my father, meaning Barrett, was a thief, and warned me against bringing 'thieves' ways' into his place. My young blood was up; I told him my mind so plainly that he turned me out of doors.

"And then for some days I wandered about, without money, lodging, or food, except what I happened to have casually offered to me by persons who saw me, I suppose, look miserable, and yet who did not see me beg.

"It was curious how the secret my mother had imparted to me on her deathbed had affected my character. While I was quite conscious that I ought not to be proud of owing my parentage to a man who had behaved so ill to my mother, and who had robed me of my rights of legitimacy (if, at least, my poor mother's story could be thoroughly trusted), still I thought so much more of the fact of his being a gentleman than of his ungentlemanly conduct, that it gave me new

motives and feelings. Could the son of a gentleman beg ? Certainly not. Could the son of a
gentleman be a thief? I tried to answer that
question with equal decision, but somehow could
not. With me dishonesty, as regarded the bulk
of the persons with whom I had been thrown
into contact, was no new fact freshly presented to
me, and which, in my capacity as a free agent, I
might judge of, and accept or condemn. No; I
had known practically nothing but dishonesty
since my cradle in the cellar. I do not think my
mother was dishonest except in one direction, the
buying dishonestly-obtained goods, but that was
quite enough to poison for me the very roots of
life.

"This particular day I had eaten nothing from
my getting up until night. I was hungry when I
waked from my hard bed in the Adelphi arches,
and I was cold ; but I had not even a copper left,
and I had still no idea of begging to get one. I
did now think of stealing; but I shrank from the
danger. I wandered along the Strand, gazing in
at every window at the treasures I saw displayed,
and thinking at times, with dry, tearless eyes, 'If
they would but give me the value of one of those
pins to live on for a few days, I would try and
go abroad in some vessel, and work for my passage, and there see if some one would not treat

me kindly, if they found I could and would work.'

" ' Move on, youngster,' suddenly said a police-man, as I was growing tender over myself and my fate. So I moved on through the Strand, and down one street to the Thames, and then up another from it, now stopping to watch the acrobats and envy them the halfpence they were receiving, and wondering whether they would take me if I offered myself, and give me a good dinner to begin with; but then the thought I was a gentleman's son put that aside, and on I went once more, without a single practical idea how I was to live through the next day or two.

" Hungrier and hungrier I became towards the afternoon, and I found myself haunting the windows of the dining-rooms outside, gazing yearningly on the hot joints within, and wonder-ing if the persons who went in with money in their pockets knew how happy they ought to be. But a stern look from the tradesman within sufficed to send me once more roaming.

" Towards dark it began to rain; but I was now in that reckless state of mind that I did not care, and so I soon got wet through. And still, hour by hour, I grew more and more hungry and faint. My courage, however, seemed strong. Boy as I was, I did not give way to grief—not, at least, while all things seemed to be bearing hardly against me. But as I stood late in the evening, in a dark passage, where a poor, draggle-tailed, miserable outcast of a woman had also sought shelter, I had some talk with her that strangely moved me.

" We had said a few indifferent things to one another about the weather, and so on, when she remarked to me, quite unexpectedly,

" ' What's the matter with you ? It don't seem right for one so young and strong to be so downcast. It's different with me. God help me ! I am just at the very bottom of all created things. But I am used to it now, and it don't matter. The doctor tells me I can't live long. But you seem hearty and able to thrive. Why don't you ? '

" ' I am hungry,' I said simply.

" ' Hungry ? Here, take a piece of this.' And, producing a roll of bread, she broke it in two and gave me half. I need not say how quickly it was devoured.

" ' Here, you may as well have the rest,' she said.

" I took that too, and ate it, thinking of nothing but the great physical relief and enjoyment.

" ' There, you've settled my supper, for I havn't a rap in the world to buy any more with.'

" 'I am very sorry,' I said, in a feeling of shame.

" 'Lord bless you, all my appetite's gone. I know I ought to eat, but I can't.'

" Somehow, before I left that woman I had told her my story, and the tears she had ceased to give vent to for herself flowed freely at the narrative of my and my mother's troubles. And then I, too, began to weep; and, once giving way, I thought my anguish would become uncontrollable. And she, poor thing, soothed me and comforted me, and bid me keep my heart up. When we parted (for she had some person or other to seek) she whispered to me,

" 'Don't think I talk about things I don't understand. Two hours ago I stood on Westminster Bridge looking down on the black water, where the lights were gleaming upon it as though it were polished marble, and—and—well, never mind, I didn't do it, so good-by.'

" That meeting was an eventful one for me. It restored my courage after a time, for I had eaten, and had caught a glimpse of a trouble infinitely beyond my own, and felt I must struggle. But I felt also a sense of how the poor and struggling are abandoned by the rich and worldly; and what little feeling of desire I had to be honest and respectable died out, and

I wanted only to be strong—strong as the men of the world are strong,. and successful as the men of the world get to be successful. But it was against them, not with them, I desired to be thus strong and successful. Even my father now seemed to be one of the host against which I should like, boy as I was, but with all the despair of a man, to make war. I am not telling you what you may think ought to have been the truth, but what was the truth—hard, hideous; but real.

" There was a fierce, inarticulate fury—a sort of second and inner self—growing up within me as I felt myself driving along from trouble to trouble, without friend or guardian, with no hope to make me bear in patience my present ills.

" Just half an hour after I had seen the last of that poor miserable woman, I was engaged in eager talk with a very different sort of person. This was a man who noticed and watched me as I began to stroll along the fronts of the superb shops in Regent-street, heedless of the rain which was driving almost everybody else to the shelter of cabs or omnibuses, the doorsteps of the shops, or the streets and passages at intervals between them.

" Presently I began to speculate on this man's appearance, life, and aims. I noticed the hard character of his face, which seemed to be incapable of any kind of mental weakness. I noticed the odd effect of his arms, which were unusually short. But the main thing was his ceaseless attention to me. What did he think about me? or what did he want with me? I had never, to my knowledge, seen him before. I grew quite uncomfortable when I found him at last, come up close to me under one of those outside gas-lamps which threw such radiance on the goods within. I fear I cannot accurately remember the conversation that passed; for I was so much engrossed—I may say so much frightened—by its nature. But it was something like this :—

"'Fine night to be out, young un, ain't it?'

"'Oh, very,' I said, laughing.

"'Valleyable things in that ere window, eh?'

"'Yes,' said I, but a little uneasily; for the man's eyes became fixed on mine with an odd and inexplicable expression.

"'Like them 'ere diamond studs for your buzzum?'

"'Y—es, if I were rich enough to wear such things.'

"'And why don't you be rich? Ain't you clever?'

"'I didn't know that cleverness was all I wanted to become rich.'

"'But it is. Are you clever?'

"'Perhaps—I don't know.'

"'Suppose you show me how clever. You see that jeweller's counter there? Look in, through this pane.'

"'Yes,' said I, though with increased hesitation.

"'Yer see the tray the man has left, with all the rings loose?'

"'Yes; but the man must be close by — perhaps stooping for something under the counter.'

"'Well, now, look you here. Nobody is watching. Slip in, stoop down, get to the counter, put up your hands and grab whatever comes first, slip out to me. I'll take the things from you, and show you how to get off.'

"I stared at the man for a moment, in mingled alarm and horror. He went on:—

"'If you're clever enough to do that you shall spend your life in clover with me. Jolly supper to-night; lots of money in your pocket to-morrow. And you may go where you like, do what you like, except when I want you.'

"'I am not a thief,' said I, summoning up a sort of heroic resolution, and turning away, with a kind of boyish pride, to leave him. But he seized my hand, as in a vice, with one of his strong arms, and made me walk along with him, though managing to avoid calling the attention of passers-by to our behaviour.

"Leading me into the first dark street, he said,

"'Hark ye, young un—think I didn't see you try to pick that 'ere gent's pocket?'

"'I? What do you mean? I didn't do anything of the kind. I won't go with you. Let me go.'

"'And of course I didn't follow you, and take all that notice of you because of what I seed? No! Well, let's see what the perlice 'll say to you.'

"'Oh! don't hurt me—don't! I didn't try to steal anything; I didn't, indeed!'

"'Well, tell the perlice so—mayhaps they're easier to conwince than I am. Well, if yer will have it,' for I was still struggling to get free, 'There, you varmint!' I went down into the gutter as if shot, by a sudden blow from him. When I got up I felt stupefied, but also full of intense rage. But he changed his manner, and said,

"'Look yer, I didn't mean to hurt yer; why should I? I took a fancy to you the moment I clapped eyes on you. Let bygones be bygones. You come quietly with me and have a good supper.   Say you will, and I won't touch you agin.'

"Had there been no secret desire in myself to get initiated into a life of successful villany I should no doubt have spurned his caresses as I had spurned his threats ; but there was a something in my mind that helped him in all his efforts to win me.

"He made me take a sandwich and a glass of wine at a neighbouring bar. The effect of the wine was wonderful. My fears seemed to die out, my hopes to become wonderfully vivid, whilst all my faculties leaped, as it were, into sudden strength.

" 'Come, that's done you good.   Have another glass of sherry.'

"I took it as if in a state of fascination from this new power, for I had never drunk so much wine before in my whole life.

" 'Now, then, let's see if I can't find yer a bed and supper for the night.'

"I followed him cheerfully. Somehow I began to say to myself, 'He does offer to help me when all the rest of the world leaves me to starve.'

"As we walked along he began to draw out of me, bit by bit, the chief facts of my history, though I did not tell them to him in the same spirit that I had told them to the poor, wretched woman in the gateway. I had wanted that miserable creature to think well of me. I now began to perceive it would be to my interest to make this man think as badly of me as I could.

"But as I advanced he retreated. He began to hesitate and to doubt, and, above all, he began to sting me by a kind of compassionate con‑tempt for my uselessness and inefficiency. The cleverness he had seen in my face did not seem to be justified by our talk, now that, under the influence of the wine, I began to speak only too freely.

"Presently I noticed that we were passing the same jeweller's shop where we had conversed together outside, and the thought flashed through my mind—'If I am to take up with him, I'll let him see I am worth something.' So I said,

"'Stop one moment.' He did stop, and I looked through the pane to see if the open tray were still on the counter. It was still there, and I saw why; the shopman was cleaning some portion of its contents.

"'Wait,' I said to my companion, ' till there is a chance, and I will show you what I can do.'

"'All right; only be cautious.'

"Fortune favoured me. A servant maid came to the door at the far end of the shop, as if with some message for the assistant. She was pretty and he careless. He stopped to chat with her. I saw that where he stood he would not be able to see me cross the floor in front of the counter, if only I stooped, and if I could cross the threshold of the shop door unseen by him. To do that I must enter the shop stooping. I glanced round on the street; there were many eyes, and some of them must see me. But I was determined to strike a great stroke at my introduction to a new career. So I said,

" 'Let me run over there and buy a cheap umbrella for you to screen me as I go in and out.'

" The man gave me some silver instantly, though watching me, as I was aware, with extreme vigilance. I bought the umbrella and gave it to the man, who instantly opened it right against the street, and stood the while on the first step of the shop, as if partly desiring shelter, and yet hesitating as to whether he would not trust himself to the heavy rain. Behind his form and the depressed, expanded umbrella I glided in, reached the counter, slid up my hand, touched some rings, heard a slight jingle, then the assistant's coming step, crawled back, met the man who was now boldly advancing with the open umbrella in his hand to thank the

assistant for the shelter, he the while getting
between me and the counter, so that I knew I
might emerge at the door in a natural posture.
But there was a cry from the assistant, who had
seen me as I rose. I could no longer pause, but
fled with my utmost speed to the obscurity of the
nearest street, attracting little attention, however,
as it was supposed I was running on account of
the storm of rain.

"The man soon overtook me, and cried out,
'This way! Stick to me!'

"I did so, and he led me through a succession
of zigzagging, short, dirty streets, and lanes, and
courts, till we emerged again in Oxford-street,
when he coolly stopped a passing omnibus, and
made me get in with him, to be carried off safely
from the hue and cry towards Mile-end.

" When we reached our journey's end he again
took my arm, saying,

"'Never seed a thing better done in all my
life! You'll do. But what did you lay hold
on?'

"I put into his hand three rings, none of them
of any great value, but 'Nobby Bob,' for so I
subsequently found my companion was called, was
delighted with this his first experiment as to my
''cuteness and sperrit.'"

CHAPTER II.

"AFTER this feat Nobby Bob professed to become very fond of me. He introduced me to his friends as his pupil, taught me to feel myself at home in the thieves' quarter, initiated me into the mystery of smoking, gave me pocket-money (though sparingly, as if in dread of my running off if I had too much), and altogether made him-self as agreeable as it was in his nature to be. And I, remembering the weight of his displeasure as evidenced by the knock-down blow I had received from him, naturally made much of these unexpected favours.

"But I was surprised that he did not at first employ me, as I had expected he would, in other robberies. For some days he seemed to let me do nothing but enjoy myself, and to waste his own time in watching me during the process, and in helping it on. No wonder the future, under such circumstances, began to lose much of the dread with which I had invested it. The stories I heard day by day of successful exploits stirred my boyish imagination. I would be a Claude du Val in courtesy, a Turpin on the horse, a Jack Sheppard if I were caught and put in prison. Even the failures, the captures and the punishments that I must hear of, were narrated in such a way that I looked at them rather in their dramatic aspect than as indications of the dangers of my own career. It was as good as a play, I thought, to sit there and listen to the hair-breadth escapes, the wonderful adventures, and the indomitable courage and pertinacity of the chief men among us. I used often in those early days to catch Nobby Bob's eyes fixed on mine with a sort of satisfied, almost triumphant expression, which I was silly enough to look on as a mere proof of his admiration of my talent.

"But I noticed also that he laid traps for me, to see whether I wanted to escape. He would take me out into the country; we would get accidentally parted—accidentally at least as far as I was concerned—and then he would meet me quite unexpectedly as if coming from a different quarter than that where I had left him. But he soon discovered that there was no danger. His judicious mingling of the fear of pain, and of the hope of pleasure, in proportion as I offended.

or satisfied him, had its full effect upon me. I was resigned to whatever of danger or suffering might prove inevitable in my career, and only too well pleased to find the life begin with so much of enjoyment.

"But these—for me halcyon days—soon ended. The moment he was convinced that I was safe he began to train me. And, although he was himself by no means one of the most skilful of the fraternity with his own hands and brain, he knew perfectly what was wanted, and how to make me develope myself up to his standard. Hour after hour did he keep me with him in a solitary room, practising all kinds of experiments calculated to fit me to become an accomplished thief. He made me pick men's and women's pockets, and under the most difficult imaginable circumstances. And now again his native brutality showed itself; for whenever I grew wearied—and he saw that I was so—he would give me a kick, or a blow on the head, and laugh if I were weak enough to let the tears appear in my eyes.

" But I need not longer dwell on this period. You can understand now my career. Remembering my first robbery of my poor mother, my first robbery of strangers on the night of my meeting with my future master and tyrant, and my last robbery, in this neighbourhood, of the Squire's plate, you can only too clearly see how I must have grown in evil, and can imagine for yourselves the tenor of the life between such events.

*   *   *   *   *   *

"But I have now to speak of a different kind of effort. I did often think of my poor mother's wishes for me; I did often speculate on the possibility of yet meeting with my own father, and then the thought would run like a burning arrow through my brain, of what it would be, both for myself and him, to be known as a regular professional thief! Fear of Nobby Bob on the one hand, and love of indulgence, which he carefully fed, on the other, caused such thoughts to come but seldom at first, and to be thrust away violently when they did come.

"But that perpetually recurring idea—I was a gentleman born—acted as a powerful antagonistic influence to the influences of my daily life and career, and at times made both seem odious and alarming to me.

"Then, too, I began to read. And, although the books and papers that most interested me were not, at the beginning, of a very wholesome sort, there seems to have been in my mind a kind of instinct which continually but unconsciously rested on better things, so that by degrees I began to have glimpses of the true nature of my vocation. Yet these were glimpses only, and appeared at the time to pass without leaving any permanent effects.

"In justice to myself I may also say that I seem to have had a strange kind of power of doing evil things without feeling the usual incentives of evil motive; and, consequently, without experiencing the ordinarily evil consequences of increasing degradation. I do not mean, of course, to be guilty of the shameful absurdity of attributing to myself good motives, or of claiming for myself moral benefit, in connection with such a career. I only mean that I was so far favoured that I never did in myself or my character sink quite so low as I sank in the everyday doings of my life. I fear you will not understand this. Perhaps I hardly express myself so that I can be understood. But you will see, from the results, that there must have been truth of some kind in what I have just said.

"It was Nobby Bob's instinctive love of violence that brought things to a crisis. One day I offended him by refusing to commit a robbery upon a chemist who had been kind to me. Angry words passed, and then one of his sudden blows. I got up from the ground in sullen silence—listened, still in silence, to all his brutal language, and, the moment I found myself alone, packed up my things, took the rail to Liverpool—which happened to be the first place I thought of—and determined I would try if I could not get on without living upon my fellow-creatures. Partly, I wished this; but I confess that the strongest motive was a fear that if I remained in the same vocation my tyrant master would find me out and compel me once more into his service.

"And now for several years I ran through a most chequered career. Every opportunity that offered, no matter how humble, for maintaining myself by honest industry, I embraced eagerly. On many occasions I took extraordinary pains to create such openings; but I soon found that habits are men's true familiars, and become, as they are good or bad, our guardian angels or evil genii. I struggled often in tears and anguish; but, amidst some self-conquests, endured many defeats.

" Yes ; I can understand well now that all this conflict of good and ill, this rousing of my passions, powers, and faculties, under the storm of trouble that so often nearly wrecked me, was, in truth, but the necessary process of purification.

"On the whole, I can now see I was advancing. I did move forwards, though slowly. My tendency was from bad to good ; yet the character given of me by all my employers was exactly the reverse. Seeing me only from their side of the shield, they thought only of my relapses. Whereas if they could but for a moment have known my story as a friend might know it; have stood with me in St. Giles's, and understood how much I had done to be with them at all, they would have saved themselves from many a wide-sweeping doubt that checked the flow of their benevolence, and have sheltered me from a world of subsequent crime, agony, and remorse. However, they worked by the light they possessed; and there are some among them whose kindness I never recall without vivid emotions of gratitude.

" Gradually my thoughts took this shape—one common enough (as a mere resolution) among men of my order—I mean during those periods when I had fallen back for a moment to my old secret ways of life. I would accumulate a sum of money—two or three hundred pounds—and then abandon dishonesty for ever. You see I wanted to make reformation itself easy and agreeable ! My health, too, began to be affected by dissipation ; and I was sometimes alarmed at the thought of a solitary and perhaps penniless sick bed.

" While I was in this frame of mind, one day, when I was about the age of sixteen, on turning the corner of a street in Birmingham, I came full face upon my old master. I knew him of course instantly, though he looked much older than I could have expected. But he did not know me. I was several inches taller than when we had parted, and had to look down upon him now as he had previously looked down upon me. Then, again, my face had changed from a boy's to a man's. My clothes were good and fashionably cut, and very different from the garb that he could last recollect as mine. No wonder, therefore, that he did not recognise me, though he looked hard at me in passing. This non-recognition tickled my fancy. I turned, overtook, and again met him face to face. He looked at me harder than ever, as though dim recollection was rising; still he made no sign till I smiled, when he knew me at once.

" Before we again separated we had concluded terms of partnership. He gave me all my own way, accepted every proposal, and laughed with something like real enjoyment, when I added,

" ' And now, Nobby Bob, I have two things more to say. First, if you lay a finger on me I shall knock you down, for I can do it now. Science, you know, against brute strength, always gets the best of it.'

" ' Werry well. And what's the other ? '

" ' Why, that I mean some day, when I have saved a bit of money, to go altogether upon a different tack. Only, in that case, I'll give you fair warning beforehand that I am going to break up the firm, and mean to do it honourably, as pals should. So, when we separate we are to separate as good friends, who won't try to injure one another because of a difference of opinion.'

" ' I accepts that too.'

" ' Then I'm your man.'

" And then began the career which only really ended for me when I met *you*, and for him when I shot him, as a midnight burglar, in the room below.

" You know the rest.

" But you cannot know, you will never know, how great a change has been finally wrought in him who writes these farewell lines since he met you on the hill after his companion had robbed you. The change may have come too late, but it is real. I may go forth from this place of shelter to be henceforward abandoned alike by God and man; but your image will go with me and will guard me—I dare to say it—evermore.

*   *   *   *   *

" And must I now stop, feeling as I do that I have left unsaid all that is nearest to my heart ? Yes, I know I must now be mute, no matter how

much else there may be that I could say for myself.

"Let me then conclude with copying from a
book you yourself one day lent me to read, a
passage which has been to me fruitful of thought;
and which was no less fruitful of hope, till the
fatal discovery was made by you of my true character—a discovery I had intended, sooner or
later, to have anticipated—and till I felt we were
no longer the same towards each other.   I know
not if it will interest you now as it did me ; perhaps even with this, as with the whole of my narrative, you may think I am adding to the wrongs
I have already committed.

"Well, of that you must judge.   Enough for
me to know my own misery and hopelessness,
even while I ask you to read both.   Farewell for
ever ! "

The passage referred to was to the following
effect :—The stains of childhood seem to drop off
naturally in the process of growth, and never
seriously to trouble one afterwards ; not so with
the stains of youth and early manhood, when the
growth begins to be arrested, and the spots to
eat like poison into existence.   Will the time
never come when the whole of life shall be one
uninterrupted period of development ?   Physio-
logists tell us that within a given number of

years every particle of the body changes and there is a new man—another of Nature's wonderful provisions for securing that purity and health towards which all her operations naturally tend. Oh, let us be sure the same process may—nay, should—go on with the mind, until every trace of the moral disease of the man of twenty shall be obliterated in the man of forty. And then may the worst of criminals not only redeem their past lives as regards others, but become in themselves innocent and happy.

CHAPTER III.

WHEN Reuben had finished his story, and read it once carefully through to correct accidental errors —which last perusal occurred on a Sunday morning —he gazed for a long time sadly on the bulky, discoloured, blurred, and altogether unattractive-looking manuscript, inly asking himself whether he should send it to the meditated destination or burn it, and so help to veil over, as far as possible, that past which he had been taking so much pains to expose. It seemed now, after all his protracted labour, so easy to get rid of the document, that the mere thought fascinated him and tempted him into obedience. With Reuben, as with so many other persons, the all-engrossing idea lost in its execution the original fervour of the conception. *Then* he had seen much good to be achieved by the task, though also much pain. *Now* that he had endured the pain, the good seemed to have faded like a sunlit cloud into the cold grey horizon, and to be no longer distinguishable. Of course this was but the natural reaction from excitement, which we all feel when we pause from great and unusual exertion. But he did not know this, and the state of his mind, therefore, seemed to him a kind of evidence of the folly of his whole proceeding.

However, he wrapped it in a large and fresh sheet of foolscap paper, and fastened it with red wax, and sealed it with a curiously antique and bulky finger-ring signet that he had found among his mother's few valuables hidden away inside her bed in the cellar, then pledged during his first boyish destitution, and subsequently recovered, and worn habitually after.

"Shall I address it?" he said to himself. "No, better not. I could not dare to write *her* name here; and if I wrote the mother's, I should feel that I had falsified my own wishes. I wrote it for both, but I thought in the writing only of *her*. I will leave it blank.

"And how shall I cause it to reach them? Let me first ask myself another question. When do I leave here, and how? Would to God I was not obliged to answer myself—but I must. I will not wait till I am turned out like a dog; yet that must be the end if I wait till the mother thinks I am well enough to go. It may be ludicrous

enough for a wretch, such as I here confess myself, to stand upon his dignity in going. But
even in that point, I may as well spare myself if
I can. No, certainly they shall not be able to
say I waited one hour longer than I could help.
I steal. even their hospitality from them now.
Well, I am able to go; I have finished this miserable narrative; I have no other excuse I can
make, even to myself, for delay, Yes, painful as
it is, shrink from the truth as I may, this ought
to be—this must be—this shall be my last day
here."

Reuben got up and walked about the room,
looking with strange interest upon every object
it contained, even the most familiar, and pausing
at each, that he might the better do so. Heavy
sighs broke from him as he went his round. Was
he consciously trying to take such a long, last, lin-
gering look of each as would enable him when far
distant to recall this room, where he had spent so
many sad and yet so many sweet hours, and
where his whole nature had undergone a complete moral revolution? He went to the window,
opened it, and gazed out. How fair and fresh
seemed the air, the surface of the heath-covered
moor, the patches of yellow furze, and the gentle,
melancholy wavings of the pine-trees! It seemed
to him, for the moment, hard and cruel that now,

when, for the first time in his life, he was growing towards a kind of harmony with their life, he
must leave them, as if Nature herself refused his
repentance, and dismissed him hopelessly from
her presence.   He had no part, he felt, in all
that beauty, and peace, and innocence.   On the
contrary, he had done his best to destroy the
peace of one who seemed to him to be but the
human embodiment of all earth's extremest
purity and loveliness.   It was time, then, to be
gone—time to have done with these vain lamen-
tations.

Would he be permitted to see Bella again?
and, if not, was he to acquiesce and go away
without the solace of a single touch, word, or
look upon which he might rest in after years,
when stricken by trouble, temptation, or by fits
of despair?   He felt inclined to cry out fiercely
he *would* see her, would peril all things to snatch
one fearful joy from her—perhaps by surprise—
no matter how, if only he could go away with a
fresh proof that she loved him even to the last.

But such wild impulses died as fast as they
were born.   He knew they could only lead him
to the brink of a precipice, where he might be
unable to stop when he saw the horrid depths
below.

If any hope of ever seeing Bella again, of being

ever again received as a friend in their house, were admissible at all, clearly it could only be in connection with the most scrupulous care on his part to show how earnestly he was determined to shun all present offence while desiring their future confidence and respect.

Still, it seemed impossible to him to take up so great a burden as daily life now threatened to be, unless he could obtain some help, some comfort, such as only she (it seemed) could bestow.

While pondering irresolutely over these things his face suddenly lightened, his attitude changed from listlessness to one of concentrated attention, as he seemed to stop and think over the new thought; then he looked at his watch, and exclaimed,

"Just twelve! They cannot be back from church before one! I could do it! I will!

"Yet stay! 'Twere better to do it later in the day—just before I start—so that no discovery may be made before my departure. Ay, and if I do so delay 'tis a hundred to one whether I get another chance. They will not again go to church, either in the afternoon or evening. Probably they will not leave the house at all, so that it must be now or never.

"Let me consider. There is the servant busy in the kitchen, and going in and out between the kitchen and the yard. The lad is at church. Matthie may be hovering about, perhaps placed on the watch by them. Though I hardly think they would fear me enough for that. No, no. Still they may have left him here for other reasons. I do not hear him talking to the servant; perhaps he is busy over his favourite sop in the pan by the kitchen fire.

"But shall I succeed? Perhaps not. The more reason, then, that I give myself every possible minute for the trial.

"And am I, indeed, in one single moment determining to relapse—to be a thief once more, and on a Sunday of all days of the year?"

Reuben's only reply to his own question was a laugh, as he set out from his bed-room on a new expedition.

He laughed; yes, and sad it is to have to say it of our hero, he did actually propose to signalise his last day—and that a Sunday—by an act of unmistakable robbery. But start not, fair reader; be not too indignant, Oh stern, male moralist—for Reuben's meditated crime may, I think, be forgiven when we know what it is he has determined so dishonestly to possess himself of—Bella's portrait!—that portrait in the locket which Nobby Bob had first stolen in the very plainest meaning of the word; which he had passed on to Reuben during their midnight talk in the wood; which Bella had re-discovered in Reuben's hands when she found him at the water side; and which, having thus led to the discovery of the piano tuner's real character, had been taken from him during his delirium by the careful and justly indignant mother.

It was strange that he should wish to get back a thing that had already been so fatal to him Nay, more, that he should run fresh risks to get it back. But no sooner had the idea occurred to Reuben than it seemed just the one thing in all this wide world that was most to be coveted, and the possession of which promised the greatest attainable happiness that his unhappy lot could afford.

He threw off his coat, thinking thus to be less encumbered, and knowing that he need not study appearances, since he must take care that he should not be seen. He also threw aside the house slippers which had been provided for his comfort in those first few days of faith in the new guest.

Thus prepared to move about stealthily and to make the best possible use of whatever opportunities might offer, he listened for nearly a minute outside his door, trying to hear the voices or movements of those who might happen to be

below. And at last he was rewarded for his
patience by hearing the servant say,

"Nay, pussy, I have no milk left for thee till
Matthie comes i' the afternoon; so you must just
drink the water or go dry."

"Very good," thought Reuben; "I know where
you are and where Matthie isn't. Now, then, to
her room."

Reuben went along with steps as soft as those
of the cat himself whose temporary deprivation of
milk had been so useful, towards Bella's room,
where he made sure the locket must be, and
where—as he felt almost with a sense of trepi-
dation—he should see much that his memory
would love to linger over ever after. The idea of
the room itself was something almost awful to
him; and when he reached it, and opened the
door, and looked into it, it hardly seemed a room,
but a kind of shrine, like a little piece of the
church cut out, and containing that glorified
saint in the window that had so much moved him
on his first visit with Mrs. Maxfield and Bella to
the sacred edifice.

How exquisitely clean, and bright, and simple,
and refined everything in that room was; from
the vase of fresh flowers on the quaint little table
at the window, to the white bed and its white
lacelike hangings, and the little hanging book-

shelves, filled with elegantly-bound volumes of poetry and natural history, with a few books of fiction and a velvet-bound Church Service. A print of a Madonna and Child hung on the wall: and Reuben, precious as his time was, could not help stopping to gaze on the exquisite tenderness and beauty of the mother's face, which almost seemed to have lent something of its own divine sweetness to Bella's countenance, just as if the latter had been accustomed to look at it through the many impressible years of growth from child-hood to womanhood, till it had become a part of her spiritual life.

He now hesitated as to where he should begin his search, or if he could begin it at all. He dreaded to touch anything of hers, even while he felt ready almost to worship each separate article because it was hers. There was in one corner of the room a green silk curtain, hanging in graceful folds; he wondered what was behind. He went to look, and saw a dress hanging there.

How well he knew it!—the pink muslin in which he had first seen her. And by its side hung the pretty straw hat. Reuben felt almost as if she herself stood there as he looked on them. These things were to his imagination part of her. Reverently he took the hem of the dress and kissed it, then turned away with tears in his eyes.

"I cannot seek it here—not thoroughly. I must not. Yet, stay! If anywhere in this room it will probably be in that chest of drawers, or in the little ornamental box that stands upon it. I will look in the box, I will open those two half drawers at the top, where she is most likely to keep gloves and trinkets; if I fail I will explore no further. So befriend me, fortune, this once! Either show me at once that which I seek, or let me go away secure of its discovery elsewhere."

He went to the box. The locket was not within; but he saw there, instead, a bit of holly-stem and a bunch of shrivelled yet still bright berries, that told him more than he dared fully to acknowledge. He had given those berries to her in the first walk they took together, and he had climbed a high bank, and through the prickly branches of an unusually tall holly-tree, to reach those berries, merely because he had heard her say with admiration, as she stood by his side, looking up,

"Look at those beautiful berries growing up there, so far out of reach!"

He went to the drawers. He opened the one to the right. It was full of delicate lacelike structures, with collars and ribbons. His ner-rous fingers felt among and between them; but the locket was not there. Closing the drawer, after restoring the contents, as nearly as he could, to their former state, he opened the other, by its side; and he thought to himself,

"It is here!" But he was mistaken. There was a locket of nearly the same size among the brooches, and bracelets, and beads that met his eye; but he was as far as ever from the object of his search.

"Quarter-past twelve! I must make haste, or I shall not leave myself time. Why, of course, when I come to think seriously, I may be sure it is not here. Her mother would not trust it, at present, out of her own keeping. She might fear it would be given back to me; she knows that I am not altogether indifferent to her daughter. She must be enlightened on that score after the burst of grief that I myself overheard when she told her mother that dreadful night of the discovery she had made about me.

"Yes; if I had not wanted to come here I should have discovered sooner that this is precisely the place where the locket is sure not to be found.

"Let me throw away no more time aimlessly. There can be but few places in the house where she would put it. It is not probable she would conceal it. She would never dream that I should do this that I am doing. Stay! Is that so? Would not the same motive that should prevent her giving it back to her daughter induce her also to keep it out of her way, lest she might ask for it, or raise questions about it, or do what I now seek to do—take it without questions?

"Two places only occur to me—the strong cupboard in the sitting-room below, where she keeps her money, and which she always unlocks herself, and her bedroom. If the cupboard, dare I force it open, at the risk of being suspected of a fresh and atrocious robbery? And, if I dare open it, can I? I'll postpone that question anyhow for a few minutes."

Reuben now stole along the passage, listening as he went for the servant, and hearing her begin to hum a lively song, then, in the middle of the first verse, remembering the day, her mistress, and what she was about, changing by an extraordinary musical transition to a slow, doleful hymn. He got into Mrs. Maxfield's room without difficulty, and might have found there many more objects of legitimate interest than he had found in Bella's, for the deceased farmer had left numerous memorials of his tastes as a naturalist all about the walls. But Reuben's eyes were content with a passing glance at one little glass cabinet filled with the most beautiful butterflies, and scarcely saw that there was anything at all peculiar in the place.

And certainly he made up here for his moderation in the other room. Drawers were ransacked through and through, one after another; locked or unlocked made little difference, for, with a bit of magical wire that he carried about in his pockets (as if needed for his vocation as a piano-tuner), he ·laughed at the intricacies of all Mrs. Maxfield's defences. That bit of wire was his only key, but he needed no other. He bent it now this way, now that, shortened or lengthened the bends, and every bolt flew before his skilful touch and that irresistible bit of wire.

But still the locket was not found. So Reuben overhauled the boxes, the store of which he verily thought inexhaustible. They were ranged against the windows as ottomans. They formed in one corner, piled one upon another, a table with a handsome cloth over them hanging to the ground. Others he fetched out from under the bed. Still no locket. He began now to think with dismay that perhaps, after all, Mrs. Maxfield had it in her pocket.

"Fool!" he cried, "not to think of that before. Of course she has. No matter, I'll hunt to the last minute. A quarter to one. Fifteen minutes only left.

"Dare I break open the safe? Why not, when I know that I don't mean to touch her money; that no temptation that I can just now even conceive of would induce me to touch it?

"Besides, she will never know of my search there if the locket be not there for me to take away. And, if it be, why then she can make no mistake as to my notions. The money safe, the locket gone, will surely tell the story to the dullest and most suspicious of minds."

Reuben ran back to his own room to get a little tool that also seemed to belong to his alleged vocation of pianoforte-tuner, but really was fitted for quite other purposes. He had left it in his coat pocket. As he obtained and held it in his hand he went to the window to look in the direction of the church, when he exclaimed,

"Here they are! I can just see them stopping to speak to a villager. Quick, then, or I shall be too late. Fortunately, if the locket be there where I suppose, I am safe for the day, as she never unlocks that place on a Sunday."

He ran down the stairs with noiseless steps, but was obliged to stop when actually within sight of the sitting-room door, because the servant was in the passage outside the kitchen, where she would see him pass. After a delay of a half minute or so, which seemed to him almost half an hour, she moved into the kitchen and left the way free.

His heart began to beat now a little painfully against his breast at the thought of the possibility of his being seen by Mrs. Maxfield and Bella opening the cupboard before it might be possible for them to learn also why he did it. But, horrible as the danger was, it did not deter him. He had determined to regain this locket at all costs, and his old reckless habits of life made him voluntarily incur a great danger for what to others must seem a comparatively slight object.

He went to the cupboard and began operations; but, whether it was the distraction of thought and energy from the work in hand by his continual glances towards the window—that window where he had seen Nobby Bob enter on his midnight and fatal errand—or whether it was that he grew nervous at the aspect of the danger that he persisted in confronting, he found the lock resist all his efforts to open it.

He paused, wiped the perspiration from his brow and from his hand, so that he might get firmer hold of his tools, then said, "If I fail this time I must go away. They will be upon me in another minute." Again he tried, and again, and each time failed; yet a third effort did he make, and the bolt flew back. He stepped in. There was a sound of opening and shutting drawers— the clink of gold accidentally moved—and he came forth, flushed yet trembling, with the locket in his hand.

"Mine once more! Thank God!"

He was yet scarcely half way up the stairs when Mrs. Maxfield came to the bottom with Bella, and passed on into the sitting-room, saying aloud,

"Is the dinner ready?" and then, in a lower voice, "Has all been quiet upstairs?"

Reuben could not but pause to hear the answer, and to smile at it.

"Bin as still as a mouse, Mem. I think he must hae dropped asleep, he bin so very quiet."

CHAPTER IV.

DINNER, tea, and supper were sent up as usual to Reuben (as if he were still too much of an invalid to come down), and then he could hear through the door of his room, which he had opened wide, Mrs. Maxfield's voice in prayer. He was more troubled than he liked to acknowledge that she had not even on that night asked him to join them at their devotions. The fact seemed to show how utterly he had passed beyond the pale even of her Christian sympathies. He did not stop to think how painful such an interview must have been to them all, how destructive of the object of the time, unless, indeed, they were all united in one common and highly elevated religious feeling, which they were not. He forgot, too, that they did not know of his purpose, did not therefore know that this was his last Sunday night with them, however impatient they might be of his stay, or however ready to suppose his visit was nearly ended.

He waited now for the deep silence of midnight to take his departure. He had given up all hope of seeing Bella again. Every scheme he formed for accomplishing this was dismissed almost as soon as thought of, for each one promised only additional humiliation, if they refused to lend themselves to his wishes. No; better leave things as they were, and make the best of them. He had got the locket—the representative of her —and he knew she had got that first gift of his, the bit of holly with its red berries. Might he not rest upon these facts, and begin his new career, and achieve a position, and accumulate money, and make restitution for all the wrong he had done, and then come back to her and proudly avow his love, and his belief that he was not less worthy of her than those who had never sinned, because never been submitted to his cruel early experience? Yes, that was his threefold idea— repentance, reform, restitution—and then to claim his rights as a man.

He began to collect what few things he had there belonging to him, and which had noticeably increased since his arrival, partly through pur- chases he had made with his occasional earnings as a piano-tuner in the neighbourhood, partly

through gifts from Mrs. Maxfield, which he did
not think it necessary or wise to return now upon
her hands, as if in resentment. Among these gifts
was a black leather bag, which she had purchased
for him, to use partly in her own service in going
to the neighbouring town of Radford. Into the
bag he now put whatever he did not carry about
him. At first he had put the locket into its old
place, the secret pocket inside his vest; but now,
near midnight, as he stood ruminating painfully
upon all kinds of topics, swayed by a thousand
agitating feelings, he suddenly remembered how
the locket had been taken from that place of
deposit while he had been ill, and therefore that
it was exactly where it would be again looked for
if missed.

He did not exactly like the idea of any kind of
contest for the possession of this locket, and yet
he felt within him a resolution that nothing but
superior force could regain it, and that it should
not again leave him while he lived to resist the
demand for its restoration.

But how should he leave the house? The
locks and bolts of the street door in the porch
would scarcely be undone without awaking some
one in the house by the noise. The bolts were,
in fact, particularly hard and unmanageable, as
he had often found when shutting up instead of

LIBRARY
UNIVERSITY OF ILLINOIS

Mrs. Maxfield. Yet there was no other way out of the house except by the windows. Could he descend that way ? He laughed at the moment's doubt. Of course he could. With a knotted rope, made, if necessary, of the sheets simply passed round a chair at the window, so that he could hold both ends close by the top against the chair and descend from knot to knot, he had managed to descend from much more lofty heights, and with less help outside ; for he saw there was a projection here half way down where he could rest, and lay hold of the brickwork and then drop to the ground in safety, having previously let go one of the ends of his rope and drawn it through so that he might from the ground throw it back through the window rolled up, and thus leave no external indications to excite the comments of passers by.

Still he did not like this way of going. Already he began to be afraid of his own furtive skill, and to be desirous to forget all the arts not practised amongst honest men. But he must do this or face Mrs. Maxfield and Bella boldly, say he was going, and then take the consequences, if Bella was, as he feared she then would be, cold and reticent, and the mother haughty and contemptuous. He knew this was the true and manly course, and he would have adopted it but for two reasons—his lack of courage again to see Bella in the presence of her mother, and a certain active fear about claims on the locket, which he was determined to carry off.

Apparently they had not discovered its abstraction. All seemed as quiet as usual at such a time and on such a night, when Reuben heard the church clock strike twelve. He began now his final preparations. He had found an old rope stowed away in the little cupboard where he had discovered the account-books, and so a supply of paper for his MS. But was it strong enough to bear him? He threw one end over the top of his bedstead, and then hung by the two ends, and even swung himself once or twice violently to and fro. The rope remained unbroken. He now placed one of the strongest chairs lengthways across two other chairs so that he could go under it and between the two supporters, in order to test the strength of its back. The rails bore him without breaking.

He now thought he would let his bag down to the ground first, so that he might not be encumbered; and as he was about to do so he fancied he heard, for the first time, some movement in the house; and then, still thinking of his precious locket, he thought perhaps he would be disturbed and met, and taxed with the possession of Bella's portrait: and then, without reflecting further, he took it from his vest and slipped it into an inner pocket of the bag, so that he might not even be tempted into giving it up by having it too close at hand.

Slinging the bag on his rope, he lowered it to the ground, let one end go, and then drew the other end of the rope up. He listened now in deep, almost breathless silence, but heard nothing to confirm his previous suspicion. He now placed the chair against the window, passed the rope round three rails, and let the ends hang outside the window. With one last look of deep affection at his room, he got out upon the window-sill and lowered the sash so as to prevent the chair from being drawn from its position. While he was lowering himself from the window by the aid of the rope with extreme care, in order that he might make no noise, he heard the bolts of the door being undone, and guessed that his movements were discovered. It was but the work of a single instant to know what he would do. He would not go back, as if ashamed; he would descend and confront them, if they really were watching him.

A moment later and he was face to face with Mrs. Maxfield, Bella, and the servant, the latter carrying a lantern.

"So, this is your gratitude—your reformation
—is it? Oh you villain!"

Reuben's blood froze as he looked upon her
angry, excited face, and heard such words. But
then, again, as he saw Bella there listening—
shrouding her anguish from all eyes by keeping
herself as far back as she could in the gloom of
the night—anger and a sense of injustice swept
all other emotions away, and he said in low, deep,
tremulous, but stern tones,

"What do you mean? I beg you to pause,
and think what you have already said before you
do me further injury."

"Are you not a villain?"

"I have been, Madam; though again I warn
you it is trying me too much to exact even con-
fession by such means."

"Oh, the dignity of the pickpocket! You have
not, I suppose, been in my room to-day—you
have not searched through and through, with no
more regard to delicacy than to honesty, my
drawers—my boxes—eh? You see, Bella, he is
silent. Did you think I could be mistaken, when
I told you whose hand had been at work while
we were in God's house? *Do you know him
now?*"

Reuben gazed from mother to daughter, almost
ready to commit some new outrage upon the

former in retaliation for that which he felt she was committing upon him, but withheld by the strength of his love, and by his passionate determination to cling through all obstacles to the hope that his love should be some day accepted.

Bella, thus appealed to, murmured in tones so low that no ears less perfectly attuned to the sound of her lightest speech than Reuben's would have been able to distinguish them where he stood, so far off—

"Mother, you judge him without trial. Speak to him; perhaps ——"

"See!" was the mother's answer, as she suddenly stooped to the ground and took up the bag; "this is what he has been so busy for. This is how he repays us at the last. Trust me; here is the evidence of all I say. Let him follow me if he denies it; let him see me open in his and your presence this bag."

She went into the sitting-room, followed by Bella and the servant, and then, at a further distance by Reuben, who again saw his coveted prize threatened, and was preparing himself to play the robber by a kind of violence, if nothing less would do.

The bag was emptied on the table, and all saw there was no single article of its contents that justified the mother's passionate charge. She looked baffled; but suddenly taking up the bag, perceived the pocket—put in her hand—and lo, the locket!

It was a remarkable group that then presented itself. The mother's first exultation at the proof of Reuben's guilt rapidly fading, as she saw, and could not resist seeing, that this was not the kind of robbery she had meant, and that all her violence was more likely to re-act in his favour. The daughter, suddenly conscious of all that Reuben had done, and thought, and suffered; now blushing at the discovery, but feeling over-powered with grief, and ashamed of the wrong done to him. The servant, full of amazement, and full of sudden sympathy. Reuben wondering at the effect of the discovery on the mind of Bella and her mother, and still fortifying himself in his determination to carry off the locket, but waiting to see how that end might be best attained.

" Goodness gracious, Bella! I quite forgot where he obtained this from. The safe! Don't you be misled again, as I was. If he is really innocent, all the better; but I must now judge for myself and be quite satisfied." She took up a candle with trembling hands (for she began secretly to fear she had quite mistaken all Reuben's intentions), and went to her strong cupboard to look at her money. She was in it for some time, counting over and over, as if unwilling to believe the truth that not a sovereign or a note of any kind had been abstracted from the money kept there, which was all in gold and bank-notes. Meantime Reuben and Bella stood far apart, though able, by the light of the lantern, to see each other. He saw her once look towards him, and her lip quiver; but then she turned away, as if unwilling or afraid to speak to him. He felt that he could not speak to her.

" Well, young man, I am bound in honesty to say I appear to have been mistaken."

" Indeed!" was all Reuben could reply; and there was possibly a touch of bitter satire in the tone, for it offended Mrs. Maxfield.

" You will not deny that I had occasion to doubt you ?"

" No."

" Honest men do not thus leave the homes where they have been so long and so hospitably treated."

" Oh, mother, you do indeed speak too harshly. You said you had forgiven the past. If——"

She was interrupted by the impatient mother.

" Bella, if you have anything to say to this young man—whom you will never, I hope, see any more—say it and have done ; and pray allow me to be at equal liberty to express my mind."

" Are you satisfied—quite satisfied—that I had no intention to deprive you of anything but this ? " asked Reuben, as he felt the last moment had come.

" Y—yes.   Yes."

" Then permit me to resume possession of my own property ; " and the audacious young fellow held out his hand for the locket.

" Yours ?   What on earth do you mean ? "

And Mrs. Maxfield, as she spoke, turned uneasily towards Bella, who did not seem to care to meet her gaze.

" Mine, Madam.   This young lady once said to me, before "—here the bold Reuben's voice began to tremble, and he had to repeat the word and then stop, leaving them to finish the sentence and understand to what he referred—the discovery of his character—" before—Yes, Madam, she once said to me that she should not mind the loss of her own portrait if her father's could be recovered.   It was I who recovered both, and sent you the one while I retained the other as of my own right."

Mrs. Maxfield was so much startled by the boldness of this appeal, and so unwilling to raise any delicate questions about her daughter, that she could only say in reply,

" Well, it is not mine—it is hers—I think she ought to require its return."

" No, mother, no, if—if— " and here a vivid blush began to banish the sad paleness that had previously characterised Bella's face, " I mean it is making too much of such a trifle to contend about it. Let him have it, and let our best wishes go with it."

Poor Reuben ! before he knew what he was doing he had dropped on one knee before Bella, caught and kissed her hand, and murmured some unintelligible ejaculation, a moment after he was on his feet, snatching up his bag, and departing.

" Farewell ! " said Mrs. Maxfield, but Reuben's heart was bursting; he did not hear, he did not pause ; and presently both Mrs. Maxfield and Bella saw his shadowy form through the great window rush off into the darkness and disappear.

CHAPTER V.

SOME few weeks after the events recorded in our last chapter a melancholy procession was moving past " The Traveller's Joy," amid signs of the universal sympathy of the poor people of the neighbourhood. They stood in groups all about the inn, with their hats off, looking with eager but respectful interest on the widowed Squire. He had passed an hour before with his deceased wife on the way to the churchyard, and he was now returning home, to realise as he best could the solitude that awaited him in life till he should rejoin her in the grave.

The big landlord had caused his great chair to be moved so close to the door that there was hardly room for any one to pass in and out; and as the Squire's carriage passed a tear was on the genial face, while his little black-eyed wife sobbed audibly.

" There, there; do be quiet, little woman.
He's got enough to do to manage his own
trouble, without seeing or hearing of yours."

" But she was such a dear, good lady!" sobbed
the poor woman.

" Well, d'ye think he doesn't know that only
too well?" inquired the landlord, a little snap-
pishly, for he was afraid of being himself un-
manned.

The Squire, as it happened, unconsciously
looked that way, and, meeting Mr. Jessop's eye,
the landlord bowed with a demonstrativeness that
was quite unusual; for he prided himself on his
independence of attitude in all ordinary times.
The Squire liked the landlord in spite of this
trait in his character, which is not always accept-
able to gentlemen of his class; and he waved his
hand in his old kindly way, as if for a moment
forgetting where he was and what he was doing.
Then he drew back in the carriage, and was
scarcely seen any more till he alighted at his own
porch.

" Who was that gentleman with him?" asked
a bystander.

" His nephew, Lieutenant Polwarth," replied
Mr. Jessop, somewhat curtly.

" What sort of a gentleman is he?" continued
the querist.

"I think I'll have my chair moved back, Missus. Here, Molly!"

Molly came, running, almost tumbling, into the house-place from the back kitchen; and then the landlord, fixing his hand on the massive arms of his chair, began slowly, and with considerable exertion, to raise himself to an erect posture, and, when that was attained, seemed to breathe more freely, and to want to move about while he was upon his legs; but his habitual disinclination either to walk or to be seen walking had rendered him at last almost unable to walk. So now, as usual, after a few steps, which seemed to make the house tremble to its very foundations, he was glad to drop down in the chair which Molly and his wife had put in the accustomed place.

"What sort of a gentleman is Lieutenant Polwarth?" was the question the landlord again heard as he began to prepare his pipe and glass. He looked a little angry and flushed at being thus a second time asked a question that it was evident, or ought to be evident, he did not want to answer. But another speaker, our old friend John Plackett, now spoke—

"Can't you see, mate, that Mr. Jessop isn't prepared at the present moment of time to give you a decided answer? Perhaps he doesn't know; or perhaps, being a wise man, he sees reasons why he shouldn't speak."

"Well, but after all, I should like to know what sort of gentleman this Lieutenant Polwarth is?"

"Very well," said Mr. Jessop, "put your hat on and run up to the hall with my compliments, and say I sent you to ask whatever questions you like."

The laugh through the room did now at last quiet this village bore; but the topics raised by his questions not only set the landlord thinking, but made him wish he could himself know a little of what he felt sure would soon be going on at the hall. A sort of instinct whispered to him— "This blow will shake the old gentleman a good deal. He will begin to think of his own latter end, and then, like all sensible men, he will want to be putting his affairs in final order, even though, after all, he may live many a year when he has got everything ready to die. Indeed, it's my belief that the people who go off the suddenest are just those who are too conceited or too cowardly ever to think they must die. Stop! where was I? What was I thinking about? Oh, I know—about the Squire's family arrangements now that his wife is dead."

Mr. Jessop had by this time lighted his pipe,

and whether he was so absorbed in the thoughts that opened upon him in the track he had taken, or that his sympathy with the bereaved Squire made him unwilling to talk, he began to draw so strongly from his pipe, and to discharge the product from his mouth so strenuously, that the village gossips began to see his majestic face grow dimmer and dimmer behind those curling and wreathing fumes till he practically, for all useful purposes, disappeared.

Let us try to clear up some of the questions that puzzled the inmates of " The Traveller's Joy."

The Squire and his nephew sat at the tea-table late in the evening, now and then each of them just touching the cup with his lips and setting it down as if keeping up the form of drinking without any inclination for the reality.

They scarcely spoke. This was not the fault of the younger man, for he frequently tried to set conversation going, but obtained nothing in answer but a dry, abstracted " Yes," or a " No," or an " Indeed !" But, of course, there was nothing to wonder at in this, much less to complain of, on such a day. But at last his desires for talk were in a sense more completely met than he had at all expected.

" Polwarth, this is a melancholy day for me.

It is true, my wife has been ailing for a long time, and therefore I might have been better prepared for it. Perhaps I ought to have been; but I am not. It has shaken me."

He was silent for a minute, and the Lieutenant began to utter commonplace assurances of sympathy, &c., but the Squire did not even seem to hear him, he was so wrapped in his own gloomy thoughts. Presently the Squire resumed:—

"Yes, I have thought the matter well over, and perhaps it's as well to tell you my mind now."

The Lieutenant bowed, and felt a cold shiver running through his veins. The tone and manner did not promise well for him, he thought.

"You like the army?" asked the Squire, suddenly breaking off the thread of his conversation to take it up again in a new place.

"Yes, very much."

"No danger of your giving it up just when you may have a chance of promotion?"

"As I did, my dear Sir, in the first vocation to which you assisted me? No, I think not. But the law really did not suit me."

"Wants more headpiece?"

"Of its kind—yes," said the Lieutenant, with a half-laugh.

"And, if I give you the means to purchase

another step, can you manage henceforward to keep yourself out of debt ? "

" I am ashamed, my dear Sir, to have to answer such a question ; but, before I do so, permit me to say I am at last living within my income, even as that income at present is ; but, unluckily——"

" Unluckily, you are in debt to begin with?"

" Yes."

" Well, now, tell me briefly how much would you need simply to wipe off these debts and to purchase promotion to a captaincy ?"

" I—I hesitate to—to——"

" Come, come, Polwarth ; surely, it is late for you to begin standing on ceremony. I don't for a moment mean to say I shall do what may be requisite—probably not, the amount may be too large ; but I wish to do what I do with my eyes open. So out with it."

Lieutenant Polwarth paused and took out his pencil, as if to run up a few items ; but there was a something in his manner that implied he was not really thinking of them, but desiring to use them as a means of gaining a little extra time to speculate on the Squire's motives and intentions, and, above all, on the probable amount to which he would be willing to go. As to the motives, the Lieutenant felt sure that he was going to receive an intimation that the long-pending question as to his heirship was to be decided in the negative, and that all that remained was the settlement of the terms on which he was to be called on to resign all further expectation.

It was a critical question. The Lieutenant was a man of the world, and perceived rapidly two issues—one that, if he specified a sum not very far beyond the Squire's own secret thought, the latter would stretch a point, under the delicate circumstances of the case, to finish the business handsomely. The other was that, if he did mention decidedly much more than the Squire was inclined to give him, he would be very likely to get even less than he otherwise might, precisely because then there would be no sufficient result promised unless by an expenditure that was out of the question.

And both these questions were complicated by the presence of a third—"Was he really to accept the position about (as he believed) to be assigned to him? Would he sell, like Esau, his birthright for a mess of pottage?" "No, certainly not," he said to himself, "not if I can help it!"

However, at last he did, by the aid of his pencil, seem to come to a conclusion, though he had to wait for a few minutes before the Squire's attention again turned towards him, for the latter had—very unwisely—walked to the wall, taken down a water-colour portrait of his wife, painted many, many years ago, and began to study it as if with new eyes. But at last he replaced the picture with a heavy sigh, and said, while his hand was yet at the nail and his back towards his nephew,

" Well, Polwarth ? "

" About six thousand seven hundred pounds."

"Hem !"   The Squire said no more for a time, and when he did again speak it was only to ask,

" Another cup of tea ? "

"If you please."

And then again there was a long and deep silence ; the Lieutenant one moment half regretting he had not fixed upon a thousand more, as he fancied that the Squire was not at all alarmed or angry at the amount specified ; but then the next, growing uneasy, as minute after minute passed without any proof that the Squire might not be secretly indignant at his rapacity and inclined to give him little or nothing.

But when the tea things had been removed by the footman, more than an hour later, and they were both sitting gloomily by the fireside, the Squire rose suddenly, though very quietly, went

to a writing-table, took from it a cheque-book,
and, resuming his seat, said—

"Well, now, Polwarth, I will give you the sum
you ask, and I will add to it three hundred, to
make it a round seven thousand pounds."

"Oh! my dear Sir, how can I be ever grateful
enough?"

"Stay! I say I will give it you; but it will
be on conditions."

"Whatever conditions you please that do not
imply the loss of your—affection." He was
going to say "respect," but remembered certain
things known to the Squire which made the word
"affection," though more demonstrative, also
more natural and inoffensive.

"Well, we are uncle and nephew, and, for my
sister's sake, I am not inclined to forget our
relationship; but this gift must be the last token
of it—of such a kind—that you must expect from
me."

"You mean, Sir?" faltered the Lieutenant.

"I mean that I shall add this to what I have
already done for you, before choosing another
heir, who is likely to perpetuate the family name
and blood."

"That I feel pained, Sir, at this, I cannot
deny. Not for the wealth or the position;
but that, after I had been allowed to draw

so near to you, I should be rejected as unworthy."

"Polwarth, be on your guard!" exclaimed the Squire, with crimsoning cheek. "What do you mean by putting aside the candid explanation I have given you to find another? And one, too, that, while not true as regards me, might be so easily true as regards you? It may be a weakness in me that I do wish to have this place remain in possession of persons of my own blood. You cannot promise me that. You have no children. You are not likely to have any, after having been so long married."

"May I ask, Sir, whom you thought of?"

The Squire looked as though he thought the question a strange, not to say impudent, one, but he replied, after a pause,

"My cousin, George Polwarth, has a family, including two or three sons. He is very poor, but a good fellow, and sufficiently a gentleman. And, as to his eldest son, I hear he is a lad of extraordinary spirit and ability."

"Well, Sir, I am in your hands. Do with me as you please. Make what arrangements you please, and I will do my best to have them carried into effect with the most earnest attention to your wishes."

"That's right. I'm glad you've said that. I

shall now give you this money with less regret."
He stopped speaking and began to write.
"There," said he, a minute later, as he tore a
cheque from his book, " be careful. Don't play
with it. It will, as you have said, relieve you at
once from all burden of the past, and improve
materially your prospects for the future."

" Oh, believe me, Sir. I will treat this as
sacredly as if it came to me from one who could
no longer supplement it by additional favours.
And I shall ever think of it with the same gratitude as if no other hope had been raised in my
mind."

" Well, I say again, that's right and manly.
And I don't mind acknowledging to you that, if
you had had a son, I should have put aside all
other questions, and have left you everything as
I intended while I had the hope of your escaping
my fate—that of being a childless man."

" Indeed, Sir ! That is really so ? " said
Lieutenant Polwarth, with a strange tone and
manner, that seemed, however, to escape him
unconsciously, for he evidently spoke with constraint.

" Certainly. You do not doubt my word, I
hope ? "

" God forbid ! No, no, no, my dear Sir."

" Well, then, we consider all settled."

" Settled ? Oh, yes. Stay ! It is but a trifle ;
but really I had quite forgot my wife. Would
you mind, Sir, my talking it over with her to-
night ? "

" To-night or any other night. You don't
mean, I suppose, to speculate on her hesitating
to receive seven thousand pounds ? "

" You make me smile ; you do, indeed, my
dear Sir, at the supposition. Of course not. Of
course she will feel as I do. But I don't like
the idea of seeming to have bargained away your
favour and affection."

" But you don't really do anything of the kind.
It is I who do it, if any one."

" All I wish is, to speak to her first, prepare
her for the change in our prospects, and then,
my dear Sir, I will tell her of your proposed
bounty, and then——"

" And then I must give you the cheque ?
Very well. Women, I know, have odd notions.
You must know your own wife best. To-morrow
morning, then, after breakfast we will meet here :
and, to please you, I will keep the cheque till then."

" Thank you."

" Good-night, Polwarth ! "

" Good-night, my dear Sir ; good-night ! "

They parted at the door, and the Lieutenant
went with hurried steps, not to the drawing-

room, where his wife was engaged, at the Squire's request, in attending to the company that the funeral had brought together, while he and his nephew kept apart, but to his bedchamber, in order that he might take counsel with himself in solitude as to the new and startling chance of recovering the vanishing estates that had at the very last moment presented itself to his mind.

A chance, certainly; but one so full of difficulties and humiliations that he dared not assume it as practicable till he had well weighed it in every aspect. But as he went he could not help saying inly to himself,

"How wonderfully things do happen in life. If I had dreamed of this eighteen years ago how differently I should have acted! But is it too late now—that is the question? And if not, would my wife consent? I can scarcely believe my own senses, that such a position should occur for me. But I must go to my room; she won't come to bed for hours yet. I can there see what is to be done, if anything, before morning. I am glad I did not take the cheque. Truly, I am amazed that I never thought of this before. But then I did not see the necessity before. I made sure he would leave me all."

He reached his bedroom. He sat down in an easy chair, smoked a cigar through, lighted a second and smoked that through, and was about to smoke a third, which he had lighted, when he became too much excited, so he put down the cigar, and began to pace up and down the room at a great rate. Even this did not suffice, so he opened the window and thrust his head into the night air, and strove to get quieted by the cold. Still, in vain his efforts. He began now to murmur to himself,

"No, no difficulty whatever—at least, none that I may not overcome if she consent. But will she ? I must have her up at once. I must put it to her. Must I tell her all ? Hang me if I know how she will take it—whether she will be prudent and sensible and see her own interest, or whether, like her sex in general, she will fly off on some non-essential and sacrifice us both for an idle fancy, a nonsensical scruple, or an over-weening personal egotism or jealousy. But I'll try. She had best not oppose me ; best not take advantage of the constraint I have put on myself while under the Squire's view, who I know would have taken her part, and not been sorry, I verily believe, of the chance to do so. I do think he hates me. Well, my own love and affection for him isn't troublesome to me by its magnitude.

"Yes, I'll have her up as soon as possible. Let me see how."

After a moment's pause he began to write with his pencil these words on a sheet of note-paper :—

" Get up to me as soon as you can. I have serious matters to tell you. Say I am indisposed, and get the steward and his wife to make the best of things. You've no very great people, I think, to deal with. Make haste."

He rang the bell. A footman appeared.

" Any of the guests gone yet ? "

" Oh, yes, Sir ; a many of 'em."

" I don't feel well, John, and particularly need Mrs. Polwarth's help. Give her that note. You can say a word aloud as you do so about me, that the people may take the hint. Understand ? "

" Yes, Sir. Sorry you're unwell."

" Quick, then."

The servant went away, and came back almost directly to say,

" Everybody is *so* sorry, Sir."

" And are they going ? "

" Yes, Sir ; but they wouldn't let your lady stay to see them off. She'll be up in a minute. She is only waiting to see the two old maiden ladies into their carriage. Oh ! here she comes, Sir."

CHAPTER VI.

A REMARKABLE DISCUSSION.

MRS. POLWARTH, the lady who now entered the room, was a tall and aristocratic-looking personage, so far as her form and a certain indefinable manner were concerned. She was also naturally handsome. But there was a something in the expression of her face that was quite out of harmony with these noticeable personal characteristics. She looked depressed and querulous. And the very first tones of her voice suggested thoughts in keeping with the face rather than with the lofty hauteur of her bearing. As one looked and listened one found it impossible to resist the conclusion that her natural character and her married life had been in sad discord, and that, in all probability, she at once feared and despised her husband.

"Well, what new scheme have you devised?"

"Why, Gertrude, you seem to think and live upon schemes."

She smiled a significant smile, but made no further reply. She, however, began to take off some of the ornaments and accessories of her dress, as she said,

"I listen."

She might "listen," but Lieutenant Polwarth did not find it so easy to speak now that the time had come. He hummed an air, asked two or three unmeaning questions, took off his coat, and began to look at his moustaches in the dressing-glass.

"You know, Gertrude, that the Squire has been greatly disappointed by our having no children?"

"I can imagine it; but he has been too much of a gentleman to say or do anything that might enable me to 'know' it, as you say."

"Of course—of course. And if I refer to it now, as a great misfortune, you may be sure I do it for good reasons."

"Which I wait to hear."

"Well, I am going to surprise you, I fear."

"Indeed!"

As the word was uttered, the speaker's eye-brows rose, but rather in sarcasm the Lieutenant thought, than in any real surprise as to what he might have to say.

"Well, when I married you, something had

happened which, perhaps, I ought to have mentioned—and which, if I had loved you less, or felt there was any real danger for you incurred, I should have mentioned—at the time."

"I confess this language sounds strange to me now, and not so pleasant as it once did. I trusted then, you know; and now——. Well, never mind that. You were going to say——?"

"That I passed through a kind of form of marriage with a girl."

"A form, Lieutenant Polwarth?"

"Yes, I thought it at the time only a form. We were in Scotland. She was very pretty, I very young and foolish."

Mrs. Polwarth coughed, and, whether she intended it or no, the sound irritated her husband, as suggesting her belief that mature age had not made him wise.

"Now, d—— it, Gertrude, don't begin that. Believe or not believe, as you like; but don't drive a fellow wild by that kind of insult which he can't resent, and yet which goes to his marrow."

"Does it?" asked the wife, in a seemingly meek tone, which left the soldier for a moment unable to go on or know what next to do; so he walked about with his hands in his pockets *to keep them safe.*

"Well, I'm not going to make a long story of it, but I am going to tell you the whole truth. Upon my soul I am, and it concerns you to know it. And I'll say more. I do want you to speak more kindly to me. Let bygones be bygones. I know I have been a bit wild, but my residence here has done me good. Enforced good habits have brought me to wish for them when they shall not be enforced. Don't, then, make matters worse. You might make them better, and me too."

"And how?" said his wife, in a somewhat more genial tone of voice.

"Well, the Squire is promising to give me, instead of his estates—which are worth at the least seventy thousand pounds, and yield a clear rental of above three thousand a year—instead of this, I say, he proposes to give me seven thousand pounds, and to adopt George Polwarth, his cousin, as his heir, because he has three sons."

"And do you expect to make a better bargain?"

"I do—with your aid."

"Proceed with your story."

"I married this girl in the loose way that Scotch law permits—no witnesses, no ceremony; and I meant her honestly—— "

"I thought, Polwarth, you spoke of a form of marriage just now?"

"Yes, I know. You confuse me when you interrupt me. There is really no discrepancy. I did think the marriage a mere form, if I chose to dispute it; but I didn't intend to dispute it—not then."

"Not then! Yes, I understand."

"Gertrude, you won't make me angry again. You shall not. I mean to say—and you know I meant it—that at that time I acted in good faith, and did not ever intend to dispute the marriage."

"But, as you subsequently married me, did the girl die, or did you dispute it? You see I grow interested at last."

"She behaved badly. She was not what I had thought and hoped."

"Yes; but you might get rid of me on that plea, I fear."

"No one has ever dared, to my knowledge, to breathe a doubt upon your character."

"Well, no; I suppose I have been spared that."

"Well, then, I discovered that before we met she had lost character, and deservedly so—— "

"But I trust you were not her only accuser and judge."

"You shall be yourself judge of her guilt, when you know all. I was then studying for the law, and had gone to Scotland for a tour in the mountains during term time. Within a few months after the marriage I speak of, I discovered her previous unworthiness—taxed her with it—she confessed, and pleaded for pardon. I gave her money and left her, intending to see her no more.

" Subsequently she came to me in London, with an infant in her arms, and demanded to be received as my wife, and as the mother of my legitimate son. I have told you you should know the whole truth. It was a legitimate marriage in Scotland, if she could prove it. But she could not do so. I had secured her only written proofs in the very hour that I discovered her guilt. What was I now to do? Acknowledge such a woman, who would have made me drag about through my whole lifetime a visible burden of disgrace, who would have ruined me with my uncle, and stopped all progress in my professional career ? "

" What *did* you do ? "

" Compelled her to renounce all claim upon me by marrying another man, to whom I gave a sum of money."

" And she did marry him ? "

" She did."

" You can prove that ? "

"I can. You shall see with your own eyes the register in the vestry of the church."

"No doubt you thus effectually barred her claim for ever, poor wretch! It was a skilful stroke. I wish I had known it at the time you made me know or fancy so many other and more flattering things about you."

"I wish you had. But you would have married me all the same."

"Perhaps." This was said with an air of such profound self-scorn and abasement that even the husband was touched for a moment.

"Do you now begin to perceive what all this leads to?" he asked.

"No; though I have been trying hard to anticipate your meaning. You can hardly, I think, intend to finish by suggesting that the first marriage shall, after all, be acknowledged, the true wife and son sent for, and I be sent away, the degraded thing to which the hypothesis reduces me. You can hardly mean to tell me that?"

"On the contrary, Gertrude, I wish to have, a few years hence, such a home to offer you as I always dreamed of as alone suited to you or worthy of you."

"You are most kind: and, meantime——?"

"Meantime I want you to help me to recover

my son, and to put him in a position to satisfy the Squire that I have a lineal heir to succeed me."

"And what do you purpose to do with the mother and the wife?"

"Oh! did I not tell you? She is dead. Of course the whole scheme would have been impracticable but for that."

"Pray, when did she die?"

"Seven or eight years ago."

"I am glad it wasn't yesterday or to-day. It would have looked so very bad, wouldn't it?" There was a bitterness of irony in the tone with which these words were said that again lashed to fury the rage of her husband; but he remained outwardly calm, though his face and lips were white with suppressed passion.

There was a moment of silence, then again Mrs. Polwarth spoke,

"And how can you possibly get the boy back, and declare him legitimate, without, in the same breath, declaring me a something I will not give word to."

"I will say I was married before;—that I had a child who was lost to me through my wife's death while I was absent; but that I have found him again now—if I do find him; for there, I confess, is a great difficulty."

" But this is not a story likely to be accepted either by the world or by me. Nay, it is useless looking at me in that way; I know you, Polwarth, and am determined no longer to fear you. Listen to me. The world will, of course, accept your story at once, if you can prove the first marriage; but then it will require the actual facts, not mere assertions; and as the actual facts would unmarry me, I should be obliged, in self-defence, if you did prove them, to hold you up to the world as a villain of a deeper dye than even the world, that is so old in villany, yet knows of."

" Gertrude—Gertrude! you tax me too far. If you think me a rogue, which I do not believe I am, you cannot hold me also a fool. I should be both were I capable of so shallow a scheme as that you attribute to me. You utterly misunderstand me. You don't make allowance for my feelings in having to tell such a story. If you did, you would wait and hear all before you spoke so cruelly. Now, mark. What I mean is this :—We will be re-married privately, but with whatever securities you please to appoint. Only beware, for your own sake, that you do not, by over caution, spoil the other part of the plan. Being thus re-married, you are placed beyond all possibility of danger. Your character is safe in case of discovery, because you knew nothing of my first marriage, and because the instant you did know you demanded and received instant reparation by a new ceremony. So much for the question of character. Then, as to the future position. You are, from that moment of re-marriage, my wife, whatever becomes of the first marriage, supposing it to be tried at law. Do you follow me?"

"I think I do."

"Well, then, don't you see that, being thus safe in the general present belief that you are my wife, and in the fresh fact of a new perform-ance of the ceremony now that the other woman is dead, don't you perceive, I ask, how easily you can help me to sink all these painful ques-tions, by dealing with the matter as I pro-posed?"

"You mean it is to be understood in the world that the wife by the first marriage died before your marriage to me?"

"I do."

"And then——?"

"Why, then, if I can recover my long-lost son, the Squire will carry out his original intention, and you will share with me the benefit, precisely as if the lad were a son of yours."

"I am astonished, I must say, by your story.

I am willing to believe things are not so bad as you first made me think—that you did not intend to injure me as a part of the scheme——"

" Gertrude, I swear to you——"

" Do not, I beg you, for I want to believe you, and I am inclined at present to believe you. Let well alone. Have you thought of your difficulty in narrating all this to the Squire ?"

" Yes, but I think that if I can convince him it is true, he will accept the solution, for I know he feels it is hardly the thing to have led me to expect to be his heir so long and then to disappoint me. He doesn't like me, but he is a gentleman and a man of honour in his narrow way."

" Well, Polwarth, I will not answer you to-night. You have opened serious matters to me. What if I refuse ?"

" I shall then tell the whole to my uncle, and see what he says."

" But, in telling, you perceive that you ruin me ?"

" What can I do, my dear Gertrude ? I make you a fair offer, do I not ?"

" Ah, well, I understand. You play your cards well—very well."

CHAPTER VII.

LIEUTENANT POLWARTH had certainly thought out his plans to some purpose, for he had placed his wife in a position that rendered it almost impossible for her to refuse her help. As she lay by his side that night in bed (where he slept peacefully enough) she found herself tossing on a tumultuous sea of doubts that kept slumber off till far into the morning. If she acquiesced, she felt that she was lending herself to a deception which galled her to think of, not only because she was naturally too proud to stoop to any kind of falsehood, but also because it seemed to her that she was thus reducing herself to his moral level, which she shuddered to think was indeed a low one. She had up to this time exercised a kind of control over him by standing aloof from his schemes and by maintaining with a sort of dignity her own character, in spite of the tendency of his example to reduce her to a lower state. If she yielded now to his proposal, she felt she became his accomplice. And the very idea of that word seemed to rankle terribly in her mind.

On the other hand, there was no great offence meditated by her husband beyond the simple fact of deception. If his story were truthful, the missing youth *was* his legitimate son ; and so no actual injury would accrue to the Squire by making him believe the wife of the first marriage had died before the second marriage had taken place. It is true he might not choose, under such circumstances, if he knew them, to leave his property open to the possibility of litigation, and he might think there was such a danger. But against that minor offence to him she had to put the terrible danger to herself of finding herself no wife at all if she allowed the Lieutenant to tell his story to the Squire before going through the form of a second marriage with her. And that act cf restitution he evidently was determined not to perform unless she consented to let him speak to the Squire, and endeavour to change his present intentions as regarded the disposal of his estates. She sighed as she felt herself unable voluntarily to incur the threatened danger without previously guarding herself in the way her husband had proposed ;

and she dropped asleep at last with the determination to yield. But she had also foreseen the necessity of taking the most absolute precautions.

While they were dressing in the morning, the Lieutenant began :—

" Well, Gertrude, have you thought over what I said to you last night ?"

" Yes."

" And you consent ?"

" Yes; if you really do intend to do your very best to guard my character and position from any possible injury."

" That's right. I'm glad you say so."

" But how do you propose to begin ?"

" By speaking to the Squire directly after breakfast."

" And suppose he still does not consent to accept you as his heir ? There may be many reasons why he should not look at the business in the same way that you do."

" Oh no; he must ! He brought me here first on the idea of my being his future heir, and he has ever since been exercising that kind of control over my life which only such an intention could justify. And though I, on my part, have not been able to deny that he did this in the expectation that I should have a son to succeed me, and therefore could say little while I was not prepared to acknowledge that I had a son, yet now that I am ready to speak out he cannot in common decency refuse to reinstate me. I have no fear of his refusing."

"Very well, that will be soon tested. But it is necessary for my sake that you should condescend for one moment to look at the state of things if he should refuse."

"Why, then, matters would be just as they now are."

"Indeed! Should I be just what I now am?"

"Of course you would."

"Pray, Lieutenant Polwarth, be good enough to look me in the face and answer me frankly this very plain question. Shall I, after you have spoken, be in the same position that I am now in before you speak?"

"Oh! I understand you now. But of course the Squire, for your sake and mine, would say nothing about my first marriage, knowing it must be painful to us. Remember, I don't propose to tell him that I was married to you before the death of the woman I first married."

"I perfectly understand that. Your chances of the estates would be small, I think, if you did. But, if I do not deceive myself, you will have it in your power at any time henceforward—say in

a quarrel, and you know we do quarrel at times
—to tell me I am not legally your wife. Do I
then gather rightly from your behaviour that you
do not propose to marry me again—before
speaking to your uncle ? "

" Why, Gertrude, surely you are dreaming. I
meant it only as a last resource. If the Squire
refuses, there can be no sort of necessity for our
going through such an absurd process. Of course
you can trust to me ? "

" Very well, then ; I will myself tell your uncle,
and appeal to him for protection."

" Dear me! How dreadfully suspicious you
are! Of course I have no objection, if you wish
it. But do you really mean that without feeling
our way any further with regard to our chances
with the Squire—— ? "

" I mean, Sir, that, if your story be true and
you desire to act with common honour or honesty,
you have not a moment to lose in remedying the
great wrong you have done me. I am quite
willing to separate afterwards, if you like."

" Now, Gertrude, why do you talk in this
painful, extreme sort of way ? "

" Why do you outrage me by compelling such
talk ? It seems to me you are still playing as
recklessly as ever with every thing that I as a
woman can hold dear."

" What, merely through a difference of opinion as to what is prudent and advisable? I wish, most earnestly, just what you wish. But I dread that we shall, by such an act as you propose——"

"I propose! I thought you proposed it to me!"

" What does it matter who proposed it if it be unwise in itself? As I say, I dread that by such an act we may risk exposing to the whole world exactly that which we want to conceal."

" And your conclusion is ?"

" Well, d—n it! if you will be so exacting, I will hurry off and get a special licence. There! Are you satisfied now? And I will think as I go when and where this silly business can be most secretly got through. But will you, in the meantime (for you know the Squire likes you better than me), will you do your best to explain my sudden absence and prepare him—as well as you can—for my appeal when I get back ?"

" Very well." Mrs. Polwarth said this with a sense that all her old weight of depression was suddenly returning upon her; but she said no more. She dropped on the sofa and let her head fall on her arms on the cushions, and there she tried to forget all her trouble.

The Lieutenant, on his part, gave one vindic-

tive look at her before he left the room—a look
so full of rage that it was evident he was hopeless
of escaping from the redress she exacted; while
it also revealed that he had ventured already to
speculate on the possibility of freeing himself
from her if the Squire was obdurate, and so, at
last, of giving him some new chance in the ma-
trimonial market.

In his hurry to test the value of his new
scheme, the Lieutenant did not even wait for
breakfast, but ordered out his horse, meaning to
ride to Radford, there take some refreshment,
and then go by railway to get the special licence,
and return by a night train. We need not follow
him in his journey, which was unattended by any
special incident.

The Squire came down to the breakfast-table
about ten o'clock, and there found Mrs. Polwarth.
She did not at first notice his entrance, and he
caught a glimpse of a handkerchief pressed two
or three times rapidly and impatiently against
her eyes, so he went towards her and put his
hand on her shoulder. She turned, and seemed
confused; but when he spoke to her it was with
so much sympathy and kindness of tone that she,
remembering his own grief, was overpowered,
and gave way to a passion of tears. It was,

however, for but a minute, and then, having cleared her face and eyes, she said, with dignity—

"Pardon me. It was very selfish. It shall not occur again."

"Was it on my account?"

"No."

"I thought not; and I must say, my dear Gertrude, that I do like man and woman to give honest and fearless answers, without stopping always to consider whether or not they may be pleasant."

Mrs. Polwarth thought there was a latent allusion to her husband in this, but she made no answer to the remark.

"And is there any reason why I should not be told the cause of your grief? It seems to me it must be, at least, more remediable than mine."

Mrs. Polwarth tried to smile as she said—

"Why, you know, married people must have troubles of their own to bear—and to bear together—and a wife cannot, at least not without permission from her husband, obtain the counsel of a third person, however much she might desire it."

"Well, I am not going to seduce you to play the traitor to your husband. If you feel you cannot with propriety speak to me without his permission, perhaps he may be willing to give it. Where is he ?　What makes him so late ? "

" He has gone away for a few hours or so on a matter of pressing and sudden business, and he desired me to make his excuses to you."

" Gone away ! and without a word to me ? "

" Yes ; but certainly only for a few hours.　He will be back to-night sometime, or very early in the morning of to-morrow.　And I beg personally to assure you it is on necessary business."

" Oh ! very well, that's quite right," said the Squire, who seemed to have just the faith in Mrs. Polwarth's word which her husband could not inspire.

And there for a time the conversation ceased, while they took breakfast.　The Squire forgot all other troubles but his own ; and Mrs. Polwarth found herself incessantly speculating on the question, should she, or should she not, confide everything to him without waiting for her husband's return ?　It seemed to her that such a course would be so much more in accordance, not only with her own principle, but with her own heart and her husband's true interests.　It seemed so dreadful to deceive even in little things a man who would not deceive her, and who had just now spoken to her with all the tenderness of a father.

Still, she did not feel quite sure whether she
ought to take a step of such decided opposition
to her husband's wishes. He had told her to
" prepare " the Squire, but he certainly did not
mean by that to leave her at liberty to expose his
unprincipled conduct towards her in their marriage, which he had said he would keep secret.
And yet if she did not tell the Squire the whole
truth she felt she had better say nothing to him,
but leave the Lieutenant to carry out his own
scheme in his own manner.

After breakfast, and when the servants had
gone away, the Squire said, suddenly—

" Gertrude, my dear, I have had a long talk
with your husband, and I want now to have a
short one with you. I am an old and weak man
perhaps, but still, such as I am, you must bear
with me. There is a good deal in my own individual history and in the history of my family,
if I were to tell both to you, to excuse my desire
to leave my estates to an heir who is himself
likely to be succeeded in due time by his own
son. But I have not been unmindful of your
husband's interests. I shall give him the means
to free himself from debt and to rise a step
higher in the army.

" But now, as to you. Forgive me if I speak
as no man ought to have to speak to a wife. But

it is useless to blind ourselves to facts. Your husband is not as he ought to be to you. No, don't speak. You need not excuse him—you need not remonstrate. I don't intend you to consider yourself responsible for a single word I say. I only want to assure you of my affection and respect, and am sorry the act must take somewhat of a furtive shape. This is what I want to tell you. I shall place at your service—properly secured for your life—an annuity of two hundred pounds. But I recommend you to let me send you this as a gift as long as I live. Come, come; don't weep. Don't be so depressed. I want this to be a something to guard you against all hard fortune. You understand that I shall take care that this is secured to you absolutely—that is to say, independent of my future will or wish; but I recommend to you to avoid the possibility of demands being made upon you on the strength of your presumed right by treating it simply as a yearly gift."

"I cannot—will not—allow you to do this till you know all," said Mrs. Polwarth, with a gush of tears, succeeding a great effort of calmness and self-restraint.

"Know all?" said the Squire, with a sudden lightening of his glance, as he saw there was special meaning in her words.

"Yes; you are too good—too noble—to be deceived. But, if I violate what ought to be the reserve due to my husband, I ask you, who show me such friendship, to advise me how I ought to proceed; for I am indeed truly miserable."

"Come, then, confide to me whatever you can."

"My husband told me last night that he had been married before he married me."

"What!" exclaimed the Squire, in a loud and startled tone.

"That he had a child—a son——"

"H'm!" ejaculated the Squire. And as the agitated woman heard the tone she felt truly thankful that he could not, at all events, believe *her* to be a party to any attempted trick upon him—not now that she was confessing what had evidently been intended to be kept back.

"And that she wronged him in the worst way —that, in fact, her character had been bad before the marriage."

"And where did this marriage take place?"

"In Scotland."

"In a church, and before witnesses?"

"No; in private." Again the Squire's tone was full of significance as he gave vent to a second

"H'm!"

"Discovering this," continued Mrs. Polwarth, "he left her, determined to deny the marriage——"

"An easy and honest way to get out of a difficulty, certainly!" said the Squire, with lifted eyebrows.

"And she, unable to prove her case and conscious of her guilt, consented to marry another man, who received with her a sum of money and agreed to take care of the child."

"Upon my word, Lieutenant Polwarth!" said the Squire, as she paused.

"Subsequently he married me——"

"Not, of course, while the other woman lived?"

"Yes, though she is now dead."

"The villain! But, in Heaven's name, tell me—Does he, then, mean to say that you are not legally married at all to him at this moment?"

"Yes; but he has gone to get a special licence."

"Oh! well, that alters the case a good deal. Of course, if he does that, he does now the best he can for you. Nobody need know, I suppose, of all this?"

"No—and forgive me that I did intend to keep it secret, even from you."

"But why? Oh! I understand. Yes, I begin

to see light through this somewhat dark business.
Your husband, I suppose, thinks he has now
found me an heir?   Eh?   Well, you do best to
be silent.   Gertrude, on my soul I acquit you of
any wrong done or intended towards me.   But I
can scarcely restrain myself when I think of your
husband."

"He is my husband."

"Yes, yes.   I must not forget that.   But what
about the boy?   Stop.   This is a terribly sus-
picious-looking story.   Candidly, do you believe
in it at all?"

"I do."

"Positively you do?"

"I do indeed, though at first I felt inclined to
treat it with scorn.   But he offered to show me
in the parish register the particulars of the
woman's marriage with the man who took her off
his hands."

"But the boy?"

"I know nothing of him."

"Poor lad!   Sacrificed, I suppose.   What sort
of education could he have under such circumstances?   I feel for him, and I feel for you.
Well, come, Gertrude; I will myself speak to
your husband the moment he comes, and see you
righted."

Mrs. Polwarth's heart gave way when she heard

this.   Proud as she was, even in her abasement, she could not help falling on her knees before him, and, dropping her head on *his* knees, sobbing violently, while he soothed her with kind words, and stroked, pityingly, her fair, long hair.   And so they remained a long time ; for he felt he was doing her good, and, somehow, his own grief seemed to be lightened while he assuaged hers.

CHAPTER VIII.

A TRUE STORY COMES TO GRIEF.

THE next morning Lieutenant Polwarth presented himself with his wife at breakfast, trying to look at his ease, and smiling as he shook hands with the Squire, but conscious that his own hand trembled as he thought of the coming storm. For his wife had told him what she had done, and they had passed through a severe quarrel in consequence; but she felt strong in the Squire's support, and he felt weak through a consciousness that she would be supported.

The Squire did not now wait for the completion of the breakfast, but ordered the servants away, and began at once.

"Polwarth, your wife has told me an almost incredible story—one that I find it as hard to believe as I think she must have done."

"I am ashamed to say, Sir, it is true. Pray spare me unnecessary pain. It was not my intention ever to have made the matter known, and

if I did not myself do so there was not the remotest fear of any one else doing it. But our
conversation of the night before last compelled
me to remember that which I have always striven
to forget—the existence or probable existence of
my son, whose rights were being compromised
by my silence."

" Rights ! "

" I beg your pardon. I did not for a moment
mean to say he had rights as against your wishes;
I meant he might have rights in accordance with
your wishes, if you knew of his existence, which
rights I was bound not to destroy."

" Well, this is to me a startling disclosure. I
cannot think, Polwarth, you would deceive me—
and in such vital matters."

" I should be indeed base and foolish, for
sooner or later the truth must be discovered."

" Well, before we talk any further on that, how
do you propose to secure your wife from the possible consequences of a discovery of these facts ?
You know that your marriage with her was a
mere farce while the first wife lived, and particularly now that you are yourself the person to
assert that the first marriage was a legal one."

" Yes, Sir; I am quite aware of that. And I
have always determined that if I saw the least
danger of a discovery, I would instantly have

a fresh ceremonial. Of course, when I myself desired to expose the facts to you I was only the more bound to be prompt in guarding Gertrude's interests. I have here in my hands the special licence for a marriage, and propose this very day to go with her to a little church in a neighbouring county."

" Why not here—under my own eye ? "

" But the danger of its being known ! "

" No danger at all. I will myself speak to the clergyman, with whom I am friendly. I will tell him that family reasons render it desirable to go through a second time the marriage rite ; and as he knows you were both married twelve years ago, he cannot doubt Gertrude's character, even though he may be surprised at the position. He and his clerk are both safe men. I will guarantee that they hold their tongues."

" But there will be people in the church ? "

" Oh, no ! They can manage to have everybody shut out for once, when they know I wish it."

" And who will give the bride away ? "

" I shall, of course."

" You, Sir ? "

" Certainly. I hope I am not so selfishly wrapped up in my own grief as to be unable to perform so very clear a duty."

The Squire waited for no further consent from his nephew. He rose, rang a bell, wrote a brief note on a little table apart, and, when the footman came, said—

"Take that to the Vicar."

The servant took the note and went out. But, as he was going, the Squire called after him, "Tell John to put the horses in the carriage, and drive round to the hall-door." When the man had gone away, the Squire continued, "Now, Gertrude, as you must play the bride a second time in your life, you had better make haste, for I have told the Vicar we shall be at his house in an hour's time. We will go there to avoid attracting attention. And he has, as you may know, a private way through his grounds right to the little door that opens into the vestry. We shall thus reach the church unobserved."

Mrs. Polwarth said nothing, but rose in obedience to the Squire's suggestion, and left the two men. She looked confused, but also very sad.

"Polwarth, I wish I could see your wife look a little more cheerful. Can't you try to make her do so? 'Tis a good time to begin. Let bygones be bygones between you, if things have gone a little awkward. Both of you might date from to-day a pleasanter life."

"I assure you it is my earnest wish to do just what you have said."

"I think you will find it in every way to your advantage." The Squire could not help throwing a little emphasis on the words *in every way,* and the Lieutenant seemed to understand them, and to be not at all aggrieved by their uncomplimentary meaning. It must be acknowledged that the Lieutenant was not proud in these things, though among his men he was called "Lieutenant Lucifer," from his bad temper and haughty manners.

"I think I would not change my dress," presently said the Squire to his nephew. "It is most important for Gertrude's feelings and future comfort that we keep this day's proceedings unknown."

The Lieutenant acquiesced with a smile, though when the Squire went away to change his dressing-gown for a coat his aspect underwent a marvellous change. He set his teeth, looking gloomily straight before him through the whole length of the room, and at last broke into an exclamation that we shall not repeat. He then began to murmur to himself—

"Caught in my own trap! I had determined either to secure him or to get rid of her. I expect now I am failing in both. If I were sure of that I'd astonish them both even now. But it would be madness to refuse point blank to go to church, and nothing less will do with him."

A few minutes later the Squire came in, and was followed by Mrs. Polwarth, arrayed in black silk, and with not a single token of the bride visible in any part of her person. The Lieutenant looked at her and then at the Squire, and the Squire felt half inclined to be angry; but, remembering what he had said to the husband about going in an ordinary dress, he could not object to the same conduct on the part of his wife. This was her ordinary dress, and he supposed her choice of it now must have been regulated by prudential motives.

They drove off immediately to the Vicar's. He was a rosy-faced, portly-bodied gentleman, whose politeness, though great, was scarcely sufficient to keep down his very natural surprise that a married lady and gentleman should come a second time to be married. However, he lost no time in doing what was desired; for he knew the Squire to be an honourable and a sensible man, and was willing to stretch a point to oblige him. Of course, he was made to understand enough to show the legal propriety of the case.

" My clerk," he said to them, " waits in the kitchen. He will be silent and discreet. I have told him he may be sure there must be good grounds for so extraordinary a measure. But he has a sort of boundless faith in me. If I approve, he thinks a thing must be right. Admirable man! admirable clerk! If only he could sing better, and wouldn't mumble his words in speaking."

They all went out together through the Vicar's hall into his garden, then along a shady walk between two formally-cut hedges, till they emerged just opposite the vestry-door. They were all so much occupied with their own thoughts that they did not perceive a man, who had been amusing himself by a walk round the outside of the sacred building; and who, struck by the appearance of the party, dropped down behind a tombstone in the churchyard, so that he might not be noticed. But the instant he saw the vestry-door opened, and the party pass through and the door close again upon them, he stepped hastily up, listened for an instant, then tried the door and slipped in.

Half a minute after this the clerk opened the door, took out the key, and put it inside the lock, then again closed the door and locked it. He had evidently gone forward into the church with the party before stopping to lock the door, and hence had been taken by surprise by the inquisitive onlooker, who was no other than the tramp John Plackett—tramp no longer, but a settled and tolerably industrious workman. His wife had that morning been so unusually bitter and troublesome to him—so " cantankerous," as he called it—that he had, in accordance with his custom in such cases, thrown down the last, left the unmended shoe to its fate, and disappeared to seek solace and resignation elsewhere.

He had heard the distant voices of the visitors as he listened at the vestry-door, and knew they must have gone into the church; so he ventured, as we have seen, to open the door, glide in, run up the stairs of the belfry, which opened close by, and which seemed his only safe place, and thus had escaped the clerk's observation.

John Plackett found himself in a winding turret staircase, quite dark at the bottom, but with gleams of light descending from above. He groped his way up, and soon came to a window that looked right into the church. The whole party were at the altar. John Plackett could hear nothing; and, as the backs of the Squire and of the lady and gentleman who accompanied him were towards him, he could not be quite sure what they were about. Of course he presumed at once a secret marriage, and everything he saw confirmed the idea. He did not wait for the conclusion, for he had to get out of the church while they were all engaged. So he ran down the winding stairs, opened as noiselessly as he could the vestry-door, and said to himself with a laugh as he ran off,

"I wonder what the clerk 'll think when he finds the door has been unlocked by some one inside."

John Plackett hurried off with his grand discovery to "The Traveller's Joy," where he amazed everybody by his whispered report that a marriage had been celebrated "on the sly," as he more expressively than elegantly phrased it— a marriage at which the Squire himself had assisted.

' "And do you know the bride and bridegroom?" asked the giant landlord.

"Never saw the lady before; but the gentleman is the same that was present with the Squire when I took him back the stolen property."

"What! What's that you say?" roared out the big voice of the landlord.

"I say it's the same gentleman I saw that day with the Squire. An elegant, aristocratic sort of gentleman, with a moustache—not a very young man, I think."

"Pray, what was the lady like?" continued Mr. Thomas Jessop.

"I couldn't very well see from that distance; but she didn't seem very young either."

"And was she dressed as a bride?"

"Well, no; I can't say she was. She was in black."

"And did you see the gentleman put the ring on the lady's finger?"

"No; because their backs were turned towards me."

"Ha! ha! ha!" roared the giant landlord. "Here's a pretty cock-and-bull story to bring us! A man marrying his own lawful wife! Ha! ha! ha!"

"His own wife?" said John Plackett, beginning to feel a little confused, though not at all shaken in his own belief that he had really witnessed a marriage.

"Ay, to be sure, his own wife! The gentleman is Lieutenant Polwarth, and the lady has been his wife these ten or twelve years to my certain knowledge. Ha! ha! ha!"

"Ha! ha! ha!" now resounded on all sides, and John Plackett turned as red as a turkey-cock. He stood up and demanded passionately to be heard, but it was of no use. If silent for a moment the guests could not for above a moment keep their faces composed. Directly he had uttered half a dozen words, the thought of his absurd mistake so tickled them that their mirth again broke out, and drowned his angry protests. So at last he sat down, looking as black as thunder, determined to leave the fools in their ignorance and conceit, till time should make them wiser.

"Come, come, Mr. Plackett, take your pipe and your glass, and lay aside all animosity. And if you like we'll drink the health of the blushing bride."

This again set the guests off, and so vexed John Plackett that he secretly determined never again to open his mouth on the subject of what he had seen.

CHAPTER IX.

THE marriage over, Lieutenant Polwarth began to wonder whether the Squire would or would not compensate him for his secret annoyance by recurring again to the idea of his son in connection with his own hope of succeeding to the estates.

It was curious the position all that day of the twice-married couple. The feeling of Mrs. Polwarth, from first hearing the story up to this time, had been one of deep and burning but suppressed resentment. To the many humiliations of her married life this story had added one greater than all the rest. But she saw her danger, and therefore checked as far as she could all display of emotion. But then the circumstances of the marriage gave increased poignancy to her feelings. To have to stoop to ask him to marry her! To know and to see that he would evade doing so if he could! And yet to be obliged to go on, or have the one jewel she possessed—character—lost to her; this was indeed bitter. She said to herself over and over again,

"Would to heaven I could now not only let him go but myself throw him off with scorn, and be thankful for the blessed relief. But I cannot! I should be looked on everywhere as weak, or criminal."

But after the marriage, when the terrible fears and doubts that had been raised began necessarily to subside, she found herself insensibly yielding to more gentle thoughts and desires; and once she went so far as to walk up to her husband as he sat gloomily by the window of the drawing-room professing to read, but really thinking only of his hard fate; and she said tenderly, as she put her hand on his shoulder,

"Edward!"

"Well?" he replied, but in a tone of such distant feeling that she shrank back at once, and walked away.

The Squire, who had been out of the room during this little incident, now returned, saying,

"Polwarth, I am glad to find you and your wife together, for we must now settle what business remains unsettled betwixt us. Gertrude, did your husband tell you what I proposed in lieu of his any longer considering himself my heir ? "

" He did," she replied, faintly, and almost indifferently; for her husband's answer to her one and only effort at reconciliation had made her at once more angry and more wretched than ever, and altogether careless of the worldly questions that so much engrossed him.

" Well, now, it is best to be candid. I am not prepared so far to alter these new arrangements of mine as you may perhaps expect. First, the boy may not even be living."

" Yes, Sir, that is true," interrupted the Lieutenant. " But if you will give me time——"

" By-the-bye, what age is he now if he be living ? "

" I think about eighteen," said the Lieutenant.

" What is he like ? "

" I have not the least notion. I only know I thought he was the first really beautiful infant I had ever seen. They are generally so very ugly, you know."

" Well, as I was saying, he may not now be alive; or, if he be, he may be a young man of such mind and character as would quite decide me against him the moment we met."

" I feel the truth of this; and if it prove to be so, he can but take the consequences."

" Yes, Polwarth, but it is you who will then have to compensate to him for the injury your neglect will have inflicted."

" I do not understand, Sir."

" Why, Sir, you do not surely dream of trying to discover this unhappy lad merely to use him for your own purpose if he suit, or to discard him at once if he does not ? "

" No, no; of course not."

" Very well. You see, then, that if he disappoints me it will be a very different thing from his disappointing you. Upon me he has at the best but a shadowy, distant kind of claim; upon you he has the greatest claims that one human being can have upon another."

" But may I ask, Sir, to what all this tends ? "

" Certainly. It tends to show that if I allow you to expect anything more from me I shall expect in return that you undertake to do your duty to this boy if you find him, and then perceive that I cannot receive him as my future heir."

Here was a new prospect for the Lieutenant— one that he had scarcely thought of for a single instant. " Probably, after all," he said to himsslf, " he is only punishing me in a quiet sort of way; perhaps he means only now to make me find this brat, and then leave him on my hands.

'Pon my life, I begin to wish I had left things as they were."

But, as it was too late for that now, the Lieutenant said, with as good a grace as he could command,

"Rest assured, Sir, I will do my best for him—— "

" Even—— ? "

" Even if you reject him."

" Very well.   Listen then.   I will give you six months within which to find and to present to me that son of yours.   During that time I will say nothing to George Polwarth.   Fortunately, I have not yet spoken to him, so I shall not disappoint him by this arrangement."

" Then permit me to say that I do feel you are acting most nobly towards me and my son ; and that, if he be found and prove worthy your affection——"

" If it be so I shall indeed esteem myself fortunate.   And now let that part of the subject drop.   How will you proceed to discover him ? "

" Heaven only knows.   But I must do my best.   And if six months should not prove quite adequate——"

" Polwarth ; I have said my say."

" I beg your pardon ; it is quite true.   Within

six months, then, I will bring him to you, or resign all further claim.   But in that case——"

"In that case?   Oh, I understand!   Yes, in that case, we revert to the last arrangement. You shall have the seven thousand pounds."

"Thank you! thank you! I desire nothing more."

"Well, now take your wife's hand, and promise her and me that as a man you will respect your new engagement to love and cherish her.   She is worthy of both."

"She is; I own that."

"Edward," said the agitated wife for the second time, "if—if——" but she could say no more.   He came to her, wound one arm round her waist, drew her to him, kissed her, and she leaned on his shoulder weeping once more tears that were not all of grief.

CHAPTER X.

On the whole, Lieutenant Polwarth reviewed with considerable satisfaction the proceedings of the day that had witnessed this renewed bond to his wife. His fear of the weakness of his position being taken advantage of by the Squire in the interests of his wife, without any corresponding benefit to himself, no longer disturbed his cooler judgment; and he felt that his uncle had behaved handsomely. Even his wife shared some of the overflow of his content. He chatted with her more in the spirit of their early marriage times; and seemed decidedly inclined to fulfil his promise to the Squire, and try to make their common life happier. And she, on her part, knowing that now at least she was safe in point of character and position, began to lose her ordinary acerbity of tone, and reply to his questions and remarks in an unusually amiable mood. She did not, as he had feared, exhibit the least dislike towards the young man who was seemingly destined to occupy the social position that her own son would have had, if a son had been born to her. On the contrary, she seemed to take quite a womanly interest in his fate, wondering where he could be, in what state they would find him, and so on.

"You know," she said to her husband, "we must be prepared to make great allowances."

"Oh, of course! If he's only goodlooking and got some spirit in him—some of the native stuff of the gentleman, as I am sure he ought to have—we can soon polish him, and make him presentable to the Squire and to society. And in that, my dear, I know nobody who can do him more good than yourself."

"Well, well; we shall see. What is his present name?"

"Don't know; but I should think either Coust or Barrett—that is, either his mother's maiden name or his supposed father's name."

"And where do you expect to find him?"

"Haven't the least notion in the world. All I know is where she lived some years after her marriage with Barrett—a cellar in a low street in St. Giles's."

"And how will you set to work to find him?"

"Well, that, too, greatly puzzles me. I am afraid I shall make a mess of it myself, if I begin haunting the purlieus of Seven Dials. And, I must confess, I am a little appalled at the idea of the questions I must put, the sort of people I must mix with, the familiarities I shall have to submit to, and the wild notions about my object that will be apt to spread. I shouldn't be at all surprised if there are not clever young vagabonds enough to be found there who would endeavour to palm themselves off upon me as the true man the moment they got an inkling of the case."

"Have you no certain means of knowing him if you should meet?" asked Mrs. Polwarth.

"No, I fear not. I can't at present recall any. I fancy there would be a something in his look, voice, or manner by which I ought to know him. I think the Polwarth blood would somehow assert itself to me; but all that is mere fancy, and may prove a delusion."

"I had no idea the case was so difficult."

"Difficult? Yes, it just is difficult, and un-pleasant, and possibly dangerous. However, I must do my best. The awkward part of the business is—as I said before—that one must go about, making no end of inquiries; and yet, one must conceal the facts that would give the in-quiries their best chance of success."

"Isn't there a class of persons who undertake such delicate business?"

"By Jove! so there is. I forgot the detective. Capital! Two heads, you see, Gertrude, are better than one. I'll be off to London, and put the whole affair into the hands of a clever fellow, and wait to see what he can make of it."

"You won't, my dear, say any more than you can help? I mean, you won't tell him anything you are not obliged to tell?"

"There, now, Gertrude, you are quite wrong. If you ever do employ such people, always tell them everything. They'll hold their tongues; it's their business to be discreet; so you can't err by overmuch disclosure. But if you happen, from any cause, to tell them too little, the facts you conceal may be just the missing links that interrupt the continuity of their work, and make it seem useless just when it ought to be crowned with success. Mind you that, Gertrude, always in dealing with detectives."

In his desire to give his wife the benefit of his worldly experience the Lieutenant became quite earnest; but she bridled a little at the notion of her having such acquaintances in the future, and then broke into a laugh at its absurdity:—

"I don't think, Edward, I am likely to need their help."

"No, no, of course. But now as to funds? I am cleaned out. Can you spare me a few pounds?"

"Indeed, I haven't any. How should I?"

"I thought, perhaps, the Squire——"

"Well, he did talk of making me a present."

"Can't you get a part of it now?"

"I'll try, though it's very unpleasant."

"That's a darling."

"How much will do?"

"I ought to have a hundred, at least, on account of these fresh expenses——"

"Well, I don't think he's gone to bed yet. I'll put on my dress again, and slip down and give him some notion how unprovided you happen to be."

"You are the best of women; upon my soul you are. Give me a kiss! There—be off."

Mrs. Polwarth sighed, even while a kind of melancholy smile of satisfaction passed over her face. She knew perfectly how hollow and heartless were these endearments, but the craving for love was so great, even while so concealed, that the semblance of it in some moods was grateful to her, as it was now.

When she had left the room, the Lieutenant communed with himself:—

"If she would but restrain that gibing tongue

of hers when she gets angry, and overlook a
fellow's little indulgences now and then, I should
be a good husband enough. Really, she is very
well, after all, for a wife. I don't see how I
could have done much better, if things go well
with this lad. She is goodlooking, ladylike, and
devoted to me. Yes; if she'll only mind what
she's about, I really think I will take the
Squire's advice, and become sedate and respectable, go regularly to church, subscribe to
charities, and be a model member of society.
Ha! ha! ha!

"Well, well; I must say things do look a
good deal brighter. But will she get the
money?"

To answer that question, let us follow Mrs.
Polwarth to the Squire's bed-room, whither she
had gone to see if he had undressed.

She tapped at the door. It was opened by the
Squire, who was in his dressing-gown, whose
hair looked disordered, and who had evidently
been weeping, though he looked stern at the interruption till he saw who it was.

" Gertrude! Nothing amiss, my dear, I
hope?"

" No—only——" And there she hesitated
at the threshold, feeling unable to " beg,"
and yet conscious that if she could but say

frankly what she wanted, she could hardly fail, or offend.

The Squire looked a little wonderingly, but also somewhat abstractedly, at her; for he had been suffering one of those terrible hours of depression which afflict all true mourners. Perceiving he did not speak, she again tried to do so, though her voice faltered and a painful heat began to burn upon her face.

" Edward is going off early to-morrow morning to begin his inquiries; and, if I might venture to anticipate your proposed bounty——"

" Oh! I understand; but you shall do nothing of the kind. That is your affair and mine exclusively. This is my affair and your husband's. I did not think of it, or I should have requested to have the business of providing the necessary funds."

He began to rummage in the pockets of his coat, where it hung on the back of a chair. Presently he put two or three pieces of paper into her hands, saying—

" Here are some cheques, received the other day, and which I have not yet paid into the banker's. The amount is £180. Take that to him. Let him not spare of needful expenses. He shall have more if he requires it."

Mrs. Polwarth caught at his hand and kissed

it. Her heart was too full for speaking. And then she hurried off, though, as she went, she felt in her inmost soul the tones of his voice calling after her—

"Good-night!"

CHAPTER XI.

MR. SMART.

FROM Morley's Hotel, Charing Cross, Lieutenant Polwarth sent, immediately upon his arrival in London, a brief note to Mr. Smart, whose name had been mentioned to him by an intelligent fellow-traveller in the train as that of a detective who had recently risen into notice by his skill, tact, and audacity, a curious and unusual combination of qualities, but all indispensable to the vocation.

In his note Lieutenant Polwarth merely intimated that a gentleman desired to see Mr. Smart immediately on business. He had well cogitated this matter of sending for him instead of going to seek him, and he decided that it would be more impressive in itself and more likely to keep him (the Lieutenant) free from the unpleasant company he had fancied he might meet at the professional gentleman's home, or office, or whatever it might be.

He was enjoying himself after his long day's journey over a fine cold sirloin of beef and a cup of fragrant tea, and wondering what sort of looking man a detective would be, how he would talk, &c., when he saw the door of the coffee-room open and admit a quiet, insignificant-looking person, who appeared to have a slight stoop, and to be altogether a very humble kind of personage; but whose eye seemed to look out from under the thick eyebrow like the eye of some wild animal from the forest bush, and to take in by one wide, sweeping, and rapid glance the features of every person sitting in the room. Somehow he seemed to know his man intuitively, for after a second look round the room—still with the same stoop and undemonstrative gesture —he walked straight to the table where the Lieutenant sat, and said, lifting a forefinger half way towards his forehead—

"Lieutenant Polwarth?"

"Yes. Mr. Smart?"

"That's me."

"Sit down."

"Thank you." And Mr. Smart sat down directly opposite the Lieutenant, and in such a position that the latter felt instinctively the light was upon his face so strong that every play of his features could be seen by the man.

He didn't like it. He felt annoyed, and was
half inclined to make him move, or change seats,
or do something or other of the kind. But then
that was too absurd. And the man's general
attitude was so exceedingly inoffensive and, in its
way, so respectful, that he rejected the thought,
with a half smile, as he said—

" What 'll you take—spirits or wine ? "

" Thank you, Sir, I'd rather have a cup of tea.
I don't get on with strong stuff. My head gets
hot, and then I ain't much good."

The waiter brought another cup and saucer
and another pot of tea, and was going away, when
Mr. Smart said—

" Young man, I think you may put a plate,
too, and a knife and fork."

" Not bashful, at all events," said Lieutenant
Polwarth to himself. And he began to speculate
whether he had best begin their talk at once, or
wait till Mr. Smart had refreshed himself. And
that thought led to another—" Will he talk till he
has eaten ? Perhaps not; he seems to be a very
great man—in his little way ! "

" At your service," now struck in the detective,
without pausing in his enjoyment of the viands,
and who seemed to know all the Lieutenant's
thoughts and take a sly pleasure in showing how
mistaken they were.

The Lieutenant looked round to see how they were situated as regarded the other tenants of the coffee-room, and perceived there was no one near enough to be able to listen to their conversation. So he began,

"I suppose, Mr. Smart, you don't much care about half confidences ? "

"Don't object to 'em at all, Sir, if so be as half success is what is wanted; and—if there be whole pay."

"Quite right, quite right! Your correction of my remark is legitimate, though not necessary, as I knew it must be so. And you can be depended on to keep my secret ? "

"Suppose you try me with regard to anybody else's ? "

"Smart, deucedly smart! You didn't get your name for nothing. Is it your real name, may I ask, or merely chosen as a good business card ? "

"I've no objection, Sir, to go into that, if you think it worth the charge. But I reckon my time by minutes when gentlemen send for me from my own place to consult with me."

"The d—— you do."

Seeing the Lieutenant still wasteful of his words, Mr. Smart began again in earnest at the tea and sirloin, and contented himself for the next five minutes by merely once saying, as well as he could with his mouth full—

"I can listen just as well when I eat, sometimes better."

"Hang the fellow!" said the Lieutenant to himself, a little piqued at Mr. Smart's behaviour; "How short he is. I shall never get my story out if I don't make a dash at it. Well, then, Mr. Smart, this is the case. I am heir—or ought to be—to a Squire in the wolds of Yorkshire, who is a widower and childless. I am married, but have had no children by my wife. It has naturally, therefore, been supposed that I have no legitimate children."

"Naturally! *I* should say!" ejaculated Mr. Smart, as he drained off the last of his cup of tea, holding the cup high so that his face disappeared behind it.

"But, in fact," resumed the Lieutenant, "I was married formerly——"

"Wife dead? *That* wife, I mean?" suddenly interrupted Mr. Smart.

"Yes."

"Left a child?"

"Yes."

"Son?"

"Yes."

"His name?"

"Don't know."

"Mother's name?"

"Fanny Coust."

"Would son take that name, do you think?"

"That or his mother's second husband's, Barrett."

"Second husband! and you alive?"

"Yes; she behaved badly. It was only a Scotch marriage; and when I found out what sort of a person she was, I refused to acknowledge her marriage with me. And, she being guilty and poor——"

"Consented to free you by marrying somebody else?"

"Yes."

"Which, of course, left you free also to marry somebody else?"

"Y——yes," hesitated the Lieutenant, feeling very much as if under a cross-examination about his conduct in a court of law under the lash of a sharp counsel.

"And you did marry before the other one died?"

"Yes."

"And now you want me to find the son?"

"Yes."

"That all?"

"Yes, that's all; what else do you suppose I may want?"

"Oh! I don't know. Of course you know that your present lady is, in the eye of the law, no wife at all?"

"I think, Mr. Smart, you are forgetting your own hint to me, and going out of your proper latitude."

"Not at all, Sir; why should I? If a gentleman marries a dozen wives, and keeps 'em or loses 'em all, what can it matter to me? But it does matter to me to know exactly how he stands with regard to 'em if they are at all likely to interfere with my operations. Your present lady may take it unkindly of a man like me to be ferreting about, in order to make her very uncomfortable by my discoveries."

"True, and I didn't think of it. Well, be easy on that score. I have again married her, in the Squire's presence, to make all safe. But I do not want, if it can be avoided, for any doubt to be thrown on my first marriage with her; I mean as to its being the sufficient and only marriage."

"I'll take care, Sir; and you and she may easily believe me—for nobody that I can see has any interest in questioning *that* marriage. It's the marriage with the first wife that will trouble the heirs, if such there be, who might dispute with you."

" Oh! that is all settled. If this son of mine, whom I have not seen since he was an infant, can be found, the Squire will in all probability leave me the estates."

" Not sure, then, Sir ? "

" Well, no ; because the lad may have grown up badly."

" Will it turn upon that ? "

" Yes. The Squire is pledged to me to accept me as his heir if I find my son within six months; and if, when found, the Squire is satisfied with him."

" And you know nothing about him ? How he has lived ? Under what name, or where ? "

" Nothing but this. His mother died when he was about ten years old, and that up to that time she lived at this address—a cellar in Seven Dials."

The Lieutenant handed a scrap of paper to Mr. Smart, which the latter carefully read and most carefully placed in his pocketbook. There was a pause, during which he seemed meditating another attack on the sirloin ; but he said, at last—

" Not very easy to find him."

" No ; but you shall be well paid if you do."

"Thank you.   But if I don't ? "

"Well, put the matter to me in your own way. What do you wish ? "

"I rather like gentlemen to take the initiative in those very delicate questions," said Mr. Smart, with a smile.

"Very well.   What say you to this arrangement—a guinea a day ? "

"And expenses ? "

"Yes, *and* expenses.   A guinea a day and expenses so long as you are actually engaged in the business.   Then, if you do discover him, a hundred pounds the moment it is certain he is the right man."

"Quite independent of the Squire's opinion of the young gentleman ? "

"Quite."

"And if the Squire should take kindly to him ? " said Mr. Smart, in the nearest approach to a persuasive tone he had yet exhibited.

"Well, then, I shall do the handsome thing, you may be sure of it !   Leave that to me."

"Certainly ; with pleasure.   But imagination, as the poet says, *is* a powerful faculty, and we *do* feel uncommonly tickled, at times, by the thought of the possibilities of things—the what might be. That's human nature, Sir, both with me and for my men."

"Your men! Have you persons employed in this kind of work?"

Mr. Smart looked at the Lieutenant with a kind of compassionate smile, but seemed to think it was not necessary for him to illustrate the question of his own social rank, so he said, as if in answer to his own thoughts, and not at all in reference to the obvious alarm of the Lieutenant—

"This is work that needs delicate handling. I shall do it myself. But then——" And he looked straight at the Lieutenant, who felt again how very much his face was exposed, and that he really must advance a step further. He did not want to do so. He wanted to play the generous aristocrat, without being called upon for any larger amount than would suffice to get his indis-pensable work done; and somehow Mr. Smart didn't play into his hands in that respect. The latter was quite willing to do his best—was quite satisfied, for he said so, with the temptations held out—but it was equally clear that he wanted something very much beyond any sum yet talked of before he would show the enthusiasm that the Lieutenant wished to see.

"What does he want?" he asked himself two or three times, but could get no answer. "Has he the audacity to secretly want a thousand pounds ?"   The worst of it was, that this particular sum, the only one in question or possible dispute, was also the only one that would have to come out of Lieutenant Polwarth's own pocket. Most persons of his self-indulgent nature would have cut the difficulty short by promising a large sum if assured that it would really satisfy; and contented themselves with reflecting how very well they would be able to afford it.   But the Lieutenant was essentially a mean man, as well as a self-indulgent one; and his annoyance was quite noticeable that he should have to risk being called on for a large sum in the event of his final success.   But it was necessary to his own comfort that he should not part with the detective till he had roused him into a vigorous determination to find the lad; and perhaps, after all, it might be as well for the discoverer to have an interest in the subsequent fate of the discovered. The Lieutenant thought it just possible that if when his son was brought to the Squire he was of such a mixed character and appearance that the latter would be for a time doubtful whether or no to accept him—he thought it just possible, I say, that the detective might have it in his power to promote or to retard the lad's success by his own behaviour, and by his own knowledge of the lad's antecedents.

All these thoughts passed swiftly through his mind as he sat opposite the lamp and in the full command of Mr. Smart's bright, strangely-coloured eye, and made him at last observe—

"Well, come, Mr. Smart, let us be frank, and to the point."

"That's it, Sir."

"What should you like me to promise you in the event of the Squire's being satisfied with my son, and formally declaring me or my son—for it might come to that—his heir?"

"Well, Lieutenant, you put the thing so handsomely in asking me what I would like, and the question is altogether so business-like, that I don't mind saying that I would *like* a thousand pounds."

"It's a large sum."

"I say I would like it because you asked me as to my likings, but——"

"It's a large sum," repeated the Lieutenant, argumentatively, and a little plaintively.

"It is.   Estates pretty good, Sir?"

"Y-y-e-s."

"How much yearly rental, if one might be so bold?"

"About three thousand!"

"Fine property, Sir.   I should have 'liked' more if I'd supposed it ud been so good.   But I am a man of my word. A thousand it shall be if you think well."

"I suppose that, at all events, would more than satisfy you? It would——"

" Set us all going, as if every one of us expected to be ultimately put in your place. Depend upon that, Sir."

"Very well. I consent."

Mr. Smart took out his pocketbook once more and began to write. When he had finished, he said—

"Will you oblige me by listening while I read this?"

The Lieutenant nodded, and Mr. Smart began to read aloud :—

"Morley's Hotel. Coffee-room, ten p.m., Wednesday, July 1. Lieutenant Polwarth. A guinea a day and expenses while on search; afterwards one hundred pounds certain if son discovered; and after that, again, a thousand pounds if either Lieutenant Polwarth or son inherit Squire 's estate."

" That's correct, Sir, I think ? "

" Quite correct."

" You see I have written the hundred pounds and the thousand pounds in full, not in figures ;

so that there may be no afterclaps—no insinuations about tampering with figures——"

"Surely you do not suppose I would charge you with anything of the kind?"

"Of course I don't. But I have had some queer customers to deal with—people that were wonderfully amiable and generous till they got what they wanted, and then thought I ought to be delighted with *their* prosperity, and never mind my own."

"Anything more?" asked the Lieutenant.

"The Squire's name?"

"Gorman."

Mr. Smart filled up the blank he had left with the Squire's name, and again the Lieutenant asked—

"Anything more? Do you want me to sign that?"

"Oh dear, no. I'm not afraid. We can take care of ourselves if gentlemen turn rusty and try to throw us overboard. But I don't like anybody to say—'That wasn't the arrangement,' when I present my bill at the end of things."

"Then that's all?"

"I should like twenty pounds on account, and your address, in case I want more, and you leave London."

"There's my card. I shall probably be with

my regiment, which is now at Chester, and the whereabouts of which you can readily learn if it moves, as I expect it will soon. If I am not with my regiment I shall be at the Squire's house. And there's the twenty pounds."

"Much obliged," said Mr. Smart, as he pocketed the notes.

"I don't think," continued the Lieutenant, "I shall stay here above a week at the outside ; but you may discover something in that time."

"I will try what can be done. Shall I find you here of a morning ? "

"Yes."

"Not much chance of an evening, I suppose ? "

"Well, I don't know," said the Lieutenant, laughing ; for he was beginning to think how he might best amuse himself during these few days in London.

"I shall be here at ten precisely to-morrow morning to report progress."

"Good-morning, Mr. Smart."

And so they parted ; and so began the search for our hero Reuben, who little dreamed, poor fellow, what was going on while he—— But let us not anticipate.

CHAPTER XII.

THE next morning Lieutenant Polwarth had scarcely sat down to breakfast in the coffee-room before two things simultaneously engaged his attention : he heard the neighbouring clock striking ten, and he saw the coffee-room door open and Mr. Smart enter.

But even this rigorous punctuality did not seem to be the result of any kind of effort, but to be, like the clock-operations, the natural consequence of strictly scientific laws. Mr. Smart wound himself up so as to appear in the right place at the right time with as much method and forethought as the clockmaker had exercised in his art when he caused so many isolated pieces of metal to come together, and assume in results the characteristics of a living and thinking being.

" You are punctual to your time," observed the Lieutenant.

Mr. Smart made no comment on this, but

wiped his perspiring forehead, hung up his hat, and sat down in his old place opposite the Lieutenant and began to speak.

" Made a beginning, Sir."

" Ah—indeed ! "

" Barrett killed the woman in a quarrel about the boy, and was transported."

" Is it possible ? "

" The boy then hung about the neighbourhood, doing all sorts of odd jobs."

" But—but—not—— ? "

" No, not thieving or anything of that kind."

" Go on."

" And then he disappeared. At least the only persons I can get hold of who knew, and still remember the Barretts, don't seem to have ever afterwards met him or heard anything about him. But that doesn't say much. Changes are pretty frequent in those neighbourhoods. The doctor and the policeman between 'em manage to see a good many people fairly out of the life of that place."

" You mean there's a good deal of disease and a good deal of crime."

" Yes, and a good deal of poverty and low spirits, and things that often make short work of people. I shouldn't be at all surprised to discover that the lad, now grown up to a man, may know the locality at this moment as well as I do, and perhaps be as well known in it, but certainly not by the name of Barrett."

" What was the boy called ? "

" Rube."

" Short for Reuben, I suppose ? "

" I judge so."

" And have you yet lighted on no traces of his subsequent career ? "

" No ; but that doesn't matter. I'm content with my first day's work. I'll be here the same time to-morrow. I wish you, Sir, good morning."

And, so saying, Mr. Smart disappeared from the coffee-room.

As Lieutenant Polwarth proceeded with his breakfast he was troubled by some painful thoughts which he vainly tried to drive away. He took another cup of coffee, but the fine flavour had suddenly disappeared. He picked out a delicate bit of rumpsteak from the bottom of a pie, and put a bit of it in his mouth, but found it disagree with him. He got up from the breakfast-table and took a walk through the room to look out at the window, but was sent away by the rain-drizzle, the mud, and the pervading aspect of wretchedness which the streets presented after many hours of continuous wet. He snatched up the damp copy of the *Times* paper, which no one had yet opened, and his eye lighted on some police case or other, which caused him hurriedly to put the paper down again, and cross his legs on the seat and lean back against the wall, and determine he would shape out some agreeable plan for the occupation of his day.

But there, even when he closed his eyes, rose vividly before him, in that London coffee-room, the picture of a bright, happy, girlish face, and of a graceful, agile form, and of a soft, fair hand, which had rested on his arm as he and she wandered together among the mountain streams of her native land. How well he remembered her surprise that he should love her—he such a gentleman, she so poor a girl! How well he remembered the look of awe, mingled with love, she gave him! Ah! she was indeed then pure, loving, and beautiful, and might have become whatever else he had pleased to make her.

But he had seen her purity of thought get sullied through his own conversation. He had seen her simplicity of character changing as she found all his influences quicken in her the sense of her personal beauty, without any corresponding development of beauty of soul; until at last she needed the stimulus of admiration, and, when he failed to give it, sought it in other quarters.

And then, as Lieutenant Polwarth's thoughts went on from that point, he saw, and could not help seeing, how fatal to her his connection with her had been; that, in truth, it was he who had caused the life that began so promisingly in the fair glens of Scotland to end with such horror in the noisome cellar in Seven Dials.

These, it must be acknowledged, were not pleasant things to reflect on. Why, then, did the Lieutenant reflect upon them? Because he could not help it. The position of his boy naturally drove him back to the thoughts of that boy's mother, and he felt he was being rightly punished for deeds that had happened long ago, which he had thought were altogether done with, and for which he had, with great charity, completely excused himself.

Would the boy be discovered? And, if he were, what would he prove to be like?

These questions worried the Lieutenant a good deal. What he most feared was that his son would ultimately appear before him as a homeless vagabond, living by the meanest of occupations, or else as a hard-handed, slow-thinking, dull, and unambitious artisan, with no worldly aims higher than his bench, no personal aspirations beyond the public-house and an occasional trip to Gravesend. This last picture somehow seemed of the two the most horrible.

To shut it out he went back once more to the thoughts of his poor, degraded, heartbroken, first wife ; and so, oscillating between son and wife, the Lieutenant felt quite uncomfortable; and losing all relish for his proposed wanderings and aristocratic visitings, got no further than to a billiard-table ; and there spent the greater part of the day, secretly wondering, between his looks at the marking-board to see the progress of the game, whether Mr. Smart would bring him any fresh news on the morrow.

CHAPTER XIII.

The Lieutenant amused himself on this occasion by taking up his watch as the time for the appointment approached and instituting an imaginary race between his watch, the neighbouring clock he had heard strike so regularly hour by hour, and Mr. Smart's appearance in the coffee-room. The detective won, for he was in the coffee-room just before his time, and seemed a little more personally interested than usual.

"I don't know," he began, in a low voice, for there were other gentlemen close by, at their breakfast, "I don't know that I have made any progress at all since yesterday morning; but if I have, then the news will, I fear, be more surprising than pleasant."

Exactly what the Lieutenant was prepared for in his present gloomy and anxious state of mind. The picture of the "low" artisan rose oppressively before him, as he merely said,

"Well ? "

"I thought," continued Mr. Smart, "I would give up for the present any further inquiry about the Barretts, and try whether anything could be got out of the word 'Rube;' but so long as I confined my inquiries to tradesfolk, and working men, and such people, I didn't progress; but the very moment I spoke to an intelligent policeman who had known the neighbourhood for some years, he said,

"'There was a very young fellow who went by the name of "Gent Rube," among his pals, and who, I believe, was often "wanted," but never to be found till his little difficulty had blown over. He was an audacious thief, if all be true as I have heard on.'"

"A thief!" gasped the Lieutenant, who was now indeed shaken to the very depths of his soul. "A thief!" he repeated, as the trembling fingers tried to set down the coffee-cup without any inconvenient manifestation of his excitement.

"'Gent Rube,' Sir, may not be our Rube. We'll hope it isn't.

"Then you know no more?"

"Begging your pardon, I do know a great deal more, if this 'Gent Rube' be our 'Rube.' Having got what I fancied to be a useful scent from the policeman, I went to a man who lives in the

Thieves' Quarter, and who, they do say, has dealings with the thieves, keeps their money for
them, and so on ; but, to speak of him as I find
him, I am bound to say Billy Marks is a good
and respectable man."

"Billy Marks!" echoed the Lieutenant in disgust at the sound of the name and the associa-
tions it raised.

"Yes, he's the landlord of a public-house. I
went to him, told him who I wanted, but got for
my answer, 'Hadn't the least notion of such a
person—oh! dear no.' But I am used to Billy's
way of proceeding and to his fatherly care of his
young reprobates. So I said,

"'Now, Billy, my man, you don't stand any
nonsense in business matters; neither do I.
Take my word, then, once for all, that I don't
"want" this young gentleman for any public
reasons whatever, but for strictly private ones,
that may turn out greatly to his advantage.'"

Billy turned round and stared full at me for, I
do think, half a minute or more. Then he begins
to jerk his thumb over his shoulder and direct me
to a little room, where he often sits and keeps his
.accounts. So I began to think I was going to
meet my man face to face without more ado. But
the room was empty. I sat down, and in a few
minutes Billy, having got rid of some customers

—that landlord, Sir, is a model of discretion in his way—came to me, shut and locked the door, and then and there told me a wonderful story, one that might have been told in a romance, Sir."

" And what was it ? " eagerly asked the Lieutenant; but who, in his eagerness, could not help reminding himself of his determination to stop all further inquiry if the prospect didn't decidedly improve.

" Why, that this Gent Rube was a smart young lad, whom a noted rogue and thieves' trainer, named Nobby Bob——"

" Nobby Bob ! " ejaculated the Lieutenant, with increasing disgust and increasing determination to put an end to the present undertaking.

" Yes, that's the name by which he was known among his pals. Well, Sir, this man got hold of a youth, named apparently Rube, when he was in great distress, trained him, beat him, and so caused him to run away and try to get an honest livelihood; but at last, when the boy had grown almost to a man, they met again and formed a sort of partnership, and became famous for the skill and audacity of their robberies, which were chiefly burglaries."

The Lieutenant wanted to hear no more. His mission was ended. The Squire would never receive a thief as his heir; and he (the Lieutenant) must not risk putting himself into the power of a thief to call him father! The very thought of it appalled the Lieutenant, and almost prevented his thinking with patience or calmness.

But he perceived still the necessity of inquiry; he must be quite sure that this *was* his son before he stopped the inquiry, or he would be losing the substance in his fright at a shadow. But then, if it did become clear to him that the fact was so, he did not want the fact to be equally clear to Mr. Smart, who might use it to the Lieutenant's future discomfort, either from his thinking it a duty that a father should look after a son—even such a son—or for quite other reasons promising profit to himself.

"All this is exceedingly disgusting to me, as you may suppose, Mr. Smart, though I do not for a moment believe it relates, or can relate, to any son of mine."

"I hope so, too, Sir."

"But what do you think?"

"That he is the man you seek."

"Impossible! Quite impossible! And if it were true I could never own him."

"Ah! probably not. I don't meddle in such questions."

"Well, Mr. Smart, I feel inclined to stop where we are."

"And give me the hundred pounds just as if he were found ?"

"How can I do that if he isn't found ?"

"But, pardon me, I believe he is. But I don't want you to pay me till I make that quite clear to you."

"Yes; hang the fellow," inly murmured the Lieutenant, "he has got me there. Well, if I am to pay him I had better realise full conviction." So, presently, he said aloud,

"Have you any special reasons for expressing so strong a conviction ?"

"I think so," said Mr. Smart, quietly and respectfully; and not taking the least outward notice of his victory over the Lieutenant in his threatened dealings with the hundred pounds. "Of course everything turns upon identity. If this Gent Rube is not our Rube, I shall be obliged to confess I have made a mistake and lost valuable time. But these are constant incidents of our calling. It is by making mistakes we find at last what is true. It is by losing our time that we generally end by gaining our cause.

"Well, Sir, after a career together of unusual good fortune, that seems to have won the envy and admiration of all their associates, they went down to a place among the wolds of Yorkshire——"

"What!" cried the Lieutenant, aghast.

"Among the wolds of Yorkshire to rob the house of a certain Squire; they succeeded, carried off his plate, hid it in the ground, so that it was discovered by a strange accident, and given back to the true owner."

"My God!" murmured the wretched Lieutenant, as he recalled the recollection of his own presence in the house, and his bringing in the tramp to the Squire with the recovered plate on his back—and thus was able to attest by his own knowledge the truth of this alarming discovery.

"But now comes the strangest part of the case. It seems this Gent Rube, who was a young man of extraordinary spirit and ability, had for a long time intended to give up the life of a thief and turn honest man, and that this very robbery finally settled him. The associates parted; after that, Nobby Bob, by some excess of caution, seems to have lost the plunder, then to have fancied his former pupil and companion had played him false, and to have followed him in a spirit of vengeance, found him living as the guest of two ladies, tried to rob them one Sunday night, and was met by Gent Rube and shot dead on the spot."

"But how could this terrible story, if true, be made known ?"

"Why, by an act that shows what good stuff this young fellow has in him—whether or no he be your son. He promised Nobby Bob in his dying moments to go to London, and see Billy Marks, who had property belonging to the slaughtered burglar in trust for a child. In spite of the danger from his former associates, the brave young fellow came to Billy Marks and spent a night in his house, and had a narrow escape of being murdered by the exasperated thieves, who got to know of the death of their former companion by the hands of a man who confessed he no longer belonged to the fraternity. And then it was that the young fellow told all this to Billy Marks, who at first wouldn't believe him, but at last got to be convinced in spite of himself." Mr. Smart continued—"Now, Sir, if that isn't your son, I am not sure, with all respect to you, that he oughtn't to be. We shan't easily find a better for you, after the sort of life the lad must have been condemned to."

This was a home thrust, and the Lieutenant felt it bitterly. He leaned his head upon his hands, and his elbows on the table, and groaned in spirit.

"Does the detective," he presently asked himself, " know or suspect that it was my own uncle who was robbed ?" He could not say. But this he saw plainly enough : if the young robber was really his son, then he would, indeed, have a promising subject to present to the Squire, should he succeed in finding him. Of course, he would do nothing of the kind. Upon that he was quite determined, if obliged to accept the conviction that Gent Rube was indeed his own flesh and blood.

While thus agitated and confused by his thoughts and bitter disappointment, he said,

" Why was he called by that name—Gent Rube ?"

" 'Gent' as short for gentleman—to show the general estimation of him; and Rube, as you suggested, short for Reuben ; for thieves like to make names for themselves, that shall be brief and expressive."

" He is a gentleman then in appearance and manners ?"

" I am told that a more attractive-looking young fellow, or a more aristocratic-looking one, cannot be seen in Regent-street on a fine summer afternoon."

" H'm ! " responded the Lieutenant, scarcely knowing whether to be glad or sorry at this news.

"You understand now, Sir, why I feel so confident he is your son?"

Whether meant or no, these few words seemed to come from the plain tongue of Mr. Smart, very much like an elegantly turned compliment to the Lieutenant's own blood, breeding, and person, and he was sensibly mollified by them.

"One wouldn't like to throw the young rascal overboard altogether if he be indeed what you think him."

"And if, also, he has had the manliness and honesty to change his career before being tempted by any special reasons, such as we might have suggested to him," added Mr. Smart. "Of course, it is unpleasant to think of him as what he has been; but the man who has the stuff in him to force his own way through such obstacles must be destined for something out of the common. And, as to his principle, I should say, for my own part, that I would rather trust to his honesty—if, indeed, he has really extricated himself in spite of all difficulties—than I would trust to the honesty of the most respectable gentlemen I know, if there were any chance of their being suddenly and strongly tempted."

"Perhaps you are right. But the Squire would never look at things in this way; or, at least, if he did, it would only be to persuade me I must be content to lose the estate and gain this precious son."

"Well, Sir, I don't think I need stay any longer. I shall endeavour before I see you again to obtain absolute proof that the boy 'Rube' is the same as 'Gent Rube,' and then my work will be finished. Good-morning, Sir."

"Good-morning, Mr. Smart!" said the Lieutenant, hesitating whether or not to pay him the hundred pounds, and prevent his obtaining the "absolute proof" he talked of, or let him go on in the faint hope that he might discover he had been altogether mistaken. By the time he had decided what to do, Mr. Smart had gone; and as a minute later the Lieutenant had forgotten his own resolve, we need not say what it was.

CHAPTER XIV.

FOR once Mr. Smart's mental decision seemed to have left him, as he wandered away from Morley's Hotel up St. Martin's-lane, and stopped every now and then as if in a great puzzle as to what direction he should take. A waggon of hay entering a livery stable yard crossed his path, and he stood quite placidly waiting for it to go in, instead of stepping quickly round its tail; and he amused himself by picking a tuft of hay, and by smelling it and chewing a bit, and didn't seem at all impatient at the slowness of the movement of the waggon, which continued to stop up the way.

While thus seemingly enjoying the idea of a bit of rural life in the streets of London, though really engaged in deep meditation, a new thought struck him, and there was an instantaneous close to his dawdling propensity, and he moved rapidly but unostentatiously along towards Seven Dials.

He presently reached the back street where
Billy Marks's house was situated, and where, it
will be remembered, our hero, Reuben, had spent
a memorable night—the same that Mr. Smart
had been told of, and the particulars of which he
had briefly repeated to the Lieutenant.

Mrs. Marks was behind the counter, and
scowled when she saw him, for it had so happened that she had more than once lost a valuable
customer through the importunate demands of
Mr. Smart, when (in professional jargon) he
"wanted" a guest. But he hastened to propitiate
the lady by a few well-timed words :

" Good morning, Mrs. Marks! Glad to see
you look so much better. Don't mind me. I
am here on business that, if it comes to anything, will be rather beneficial than otherwise to
the house."

" Oh, indeed ! " said Mrs. Marks, but with an
unchanged countenance, and a particularly angry
and watchful eye.

" Billy up-stairs ? "

" Yes."

" Send us up a bottle of your best sherry for
the good of the house, and a bottle of soda-water
for the good of me, also pipes and tobacco," said
Mr. Smart, with a smile, knowing what the best
sherry was apt to be under such circumstances,

and only desirous that she should use the opportunity to send her worst and charge her highest price. "If that won't mollify her, the d—— take the woman," said Mr. Smart to himself, "for she looks as dangerous as a wild beast that fancies you are looking after its young."

He went up-stairs, knocked at the door, found Billy Marks fuming over some awkwardness in his accounts, and not in the best of tempers in consequence.

"I have ordered a bottle of sherry, pipes and tobacco, for us two, Billy, and want a bit of talk with you."

"I never drink of a morning. I have smoked, and don't want to smoke again just yet; and, as to talk, I'm busy."

"Got the same notion as his blessed wife, I suppose, that I'm the ruin of their house, the disturber of their feasts, the unprincipled invader of their domestic sanctuary," said Mr. Smart to himself, as he received this rebuff; but he coolly sat down to the same table with the landlord, saying,

"You are bothered! I see it in your eyes and in the red lines across your forehead. I am a good accountant. If you won't talk let me work. I'll soon clear up your difficulties for you."

"Well," said Billy Marks, who was at once taken aback by this Christian-like forgiveness of injuries, "it's this here confounded score which Swell Jack has lately run up, and which he now wants to pay me."

"Do you trust?"

"Not many of 'em. But there's them among 'em whom I'd trust not only to pay the score, but to keep the score."

"What, thieves!"

"Well, Mr. Smart, that's a word we don't use here, and I don't like it. They're naterally a bit tender on that point. Don't do it again, please."

"I won't. I beg your, and their, pardon. It escaped me rashly. But do you mean——"

"I do mean that these very men who will fleece the world so mercilessly, won't hurt me to the vally of a bad sixpence."

"Strange, I must say!"

"Strange! not at all: why should they? D'ye think they don't want friends, and know when they've got friends, same as other people? Is the world their friend? Or the world's big bullying law? D'ye think that if Parliament men had the sense to make these men a fair offer to employ their talents they wouldn't accept it? D'ye think that if they've got children they

don't often have the heartache about 'em? What
can they do? Once a thief always a thief! Isn't
that every honest man's faith?   And then, to
complete the business beautifully, don't the
honest men take care that there shall be lots of
chances to breed thieves, and nurse 'em up in
strength and wice?"

"Well, Billy Marks, so far as I can follow
your somewhat original views, I do think much
might be done if the people in authority had but
the strength of will to say such things should no
longer be, and the sense and patience to master
all the difficulties. But how would that do for
us?"

"Speak for yourself, Mr. Smart."

"Well, it wouldn't do at all for me."

The wine and pipes and tobacco, now appeared, and stopped the conversation. But as
soon as the dirty, slipshod girl had gone away,
Billy Marks said,

"Will you have the kindness to run up them
figures? If you'll believe me I've reckoned 'em
up just seven times, and every one of the seven
made the total come out quite different from the
others."

Mr. Smart did as he was bid, and in spite
of the blots and half-erased figures, and the
mysterious shapes of other figures, he got

out what seemed the true total, and mentioned it.

"That's it!" exclaimed the landlord in ecstacy. "I never goes wrong in my head but always in my books. I'd added, and deducted, and got everything right while I kept off the pen and ink, and then everything went wrong. But you see, one can't exactly do without pen and ink. One can't say to a customer, 'Look inside my head, and add it all up, and you'll see it's right.' "

"No, certainly not," said Mr. Smart, with a smile; "and if at any time you are at a loss, and will drop me a line, I will come with pleasure to you, and make no charge. Only, mind, I won't find my own wine and pipes for us both besides."

This joke seemed so capital that Billy quite roared again, and then began to cough, for he was a little asthmatical, and his malignant-looking wife came up to see what was the matter, and try if she could not dispatch Mr. Smart. But she saw the two men were quite comfortable together, and that spectacle she could not bear, so she ran downstairs to beat the poor slipshod girl for bringing her such tales about her master looking angry and "quarrelsome-like" at the strange gentleman.

"Well, now, Billy, I am going to repay your

confidence to me the other day about Gent Rube, by telling you why I made the inquiry. He is supposed to be the son of a gentleman, an officer in the army; and it seems likely that large estates may come to him some time or other, if only he can be discovered, and his character whitewashed."

Billy Marks was obliged to make Mr. Smart slowly repeat the whole of this in short sentences, so as to be of easy digestion, before he could say, with eyes full of wonder,

" Yes; go on."

" But, first, the question is of identity."

" Of course."

" The true person was a lad named Rube, whose mother was a Mrs. Barrett, a woman who lived in a cellar in this neighbourhood for several years, and was killed in a brawl by Barrett, her second husband, she having been married before in Scotland, but her marriage not having been acknowledged by the father of ' Rube.' "

All these facts had similarly to be broken up into detail and administered a second time before Billy Marks showed he had got them safe into his head.

" Well, the father of Rube has no other son, and he wants one very badly, for the sake of a certain uncle, who is the owner of large estates."

" And if we can prove Rube to be Gent Rube, that lad will get all ? " broke out Billy Marks, at last, radiant with the clearness of his ideas.

" Well, no, we mustn't go so fast. He may, or he may not, get the estates. His antecedents are awkward."

" That's true," said Billy, in a melancholy and thoughtful tone.

" But now, can you help me to discover, beyond all question, whether or no the boy ' Rube ' is your favourite ' Gent Rube,' the young fellow you spoke so highly of ? "

" He must be ! He shall be ! I know he is ! " thundered out Billy.

" Yes—but how ? "

" How ? " echoed Billy, beginning to look perplexed about the interests of his client.

" Yes, how ? I believe as you do."

" Doesn't he look a born gentleman, every inch of him ? "

" Never having had the pleasure to see him, I cannot say ; but I don't doubt your accuracy or discrimination. But lawyers don't pay due respect to looks when they get you into a court."

There was a knock at the door.

" Come in," shouted Billy.

A man of fashionable appearance entered, at first with an easy, assured manner, which changed suddenly when he caught sight of Mr. Smart.

"A friend, Jack! a friend," said Billy Marks; and the gentleman, who was no other than our old acquaintance, Swell Jack, sat down at once, and dismissed his fear, whatever it might have been.

"I say, Jack, have you heard anything more of your friend Gent Rube?" asked Billy Marks.

"Nothing. Why do you ask?"

"He's wanted," replied Billy.

"Indeed!" and again fierce and suspicious looks were darted at the stranger.

"Yes; and, what's more, if the lad only knew it, he'd be only too glad to come!"

"Indeed!" again said Swell Jack; but with a return to his ordinarily composed demeanor.

"Caution, Billy, caution! I am not permitted to speak even as I have spoken; but I knew I could trust you," interposed Mr. Smart.

"And if it be anything to the interest of my friend Gent Rube, Billy Marks will tell you I, too, am to be trusted," said Swell Jack.

Billy nodded two or three times in confirmation.

Mr. Smart then explained the supposed connection between "Rube," and "Gent Rube" to

Swell Jack, who, however, was like everybody else—quite in the dark.

But, after asking a good many questions and looking inquisitively a good many times at Mr. Smart, Swell Jack at last said,

"I didn't mean to let it be got out of me; and if any bad use be made of what I say, it'll be the worse for the party concerned. That's all I have to say on that subject."

"You may trust me," said Mr. Smart, with a quiet smile.

"Well, then, I discovered where he was after his visit here about Nobby Bob's child."

"You did? What, only a few weeks ago? The very house where he was?" asked Mr. Smart, with unwonted eagerness.

"Yes; and I will write you down the address." So saying, he wrote down Mrs. Maxfield's name and residence.

"Come, this is quite a new start. I begin to think now I shall soon find 'Gent Rube.' He at least can clear up the question whether he is or is not the 'Rube' of the cellar that we want."

And, having obtained this precious bit of fresh information, Mr. Smart seemed to forget business altogether, and devote himself to the sole occupation of amusing his companions, who were both astonished to find how much of quiet fun and geniality there was in him ; how ready he was to sympathise with the very men whom he was supposed to think of by day and by night only as beasts of prey, to be hunted down when worth the attention of so great a man.

"Well! he's a deep 'un, that I will say," observed Billy Marks, as Mr. Smart withdrew, after the finishing of the wine, and after a cordial grasp of the hand of each of the men.

"Yes; but I'm not going to forget he's a detective, for all that ; for I know he won't forget it, should occasion arise."

"Of course.   Business *is* business, you know," sagely and placidly remarked Billy.

"Confound such business, say I," replied Swell Jack, with natural warmth, as they then began to square the account of the score.

"Shall I return to the hotel ? " said Mr. Smart to himself, as he got back to the street ; "shall I return at once and tell him what I have heard? If I do, he'll never stand it. No; he'll never consent that I shall go down so near his uncle's house. I've got an odd fancy in my brain. What if Rube be not only 'Gent Rube,' but the robber of the Squire's house—the robber of the very gentleman who now is waiting for his discovery to see if he will make him his heir ! "

That evening the Lieutenant received a note

in a strange hand, which, on opening, read
thus :—

"Dear Sir,—I have heard something which
makes me think I shall before long be able to
bring your prodigal son to your arms. I will
say no more, but that I am leaving London for
some days, and shall be unable to give you any
address. But I will write or see you the moment
I am satisfied.—Yours obediently,

"CHARLES SMART."

CHAPTER XV.

THE Lieutenant's first impulse, on reading the detective's letter—with its kind assurance of bringing the missing son to the father's arms—was to ring the bell, call for his bill, pay it, run upstairs to his bedroom, pack his luggage, and get it brought down to the coffee-room, ready for him when he should call for it in half-an-hour, on his return from a short walk. He then started off to try to catch Mr. Smart before his departure from his office, but on reaching the house he found that Mr. Smart had gone away an hour before, "into the country" for "several days."

"I want particularly to write to him. Can you give me his address?"

"No, sir; but we shall be very likely to hear from him; and therefore, if you leave any letters or messages, they shall be forwarded."

"Oh! of course. For Mr. Smart to acknow-ledge or not, as he pleases, when he gets my letters. That's no use to me!" muttered Lieutenant Polwarth to himself, as he turned away.

But he hurried back to the hotel for his luggage, determined to take the first train into Yorkshire; and, fancying he might even yet get hold of the detective at the station, or overtake him at the end of the journey if he had really (as the Lieutenant feared) gone to the neighbourhood of his uncle's residence. As he went, however, he thought to himself there would be no harm in writing a few determined lines to Mr. Smart; for he had a strong conviction that whatever he wrote would reach him, though it might be treated as if not reaching.

He sat down in the coffee-room, after a hasty and helpless look at that wonderful piece of mystery, "Bradshaw," and wrote the following letter :—

" MORLEY'S HOTEL, July 1.

" Sir,—In answer to yours just received, I must express to you my strong disapprobation of your proposed journey—taken without consulting me—and which I am satisfied is based on a delusion. The character you speak of cannot be the person I seek. I wish you distinctly to understand that I will be at no further expense after you receive this, though I shall be quite willing to satisfy all your just expectations for your trouble and skill up to the present time.—Yours, &c.,

"EDWARD POLWARTH.

"P.S. Although I think you are quite mistaken, I shall pay you the hundred pounds you expected if the inquiry be stopped at once, as a tribute to your talent and energy, but not otherwise."

This letter the Lieutenant inclosed in an envelope and dispatched, writing outside, in a very bold hand, IMMEDIATE.

Five minutes later the Lieutenant was rattling along the stones in a hansom, giving vent to sundry oaths and imprecations against the poor tired cab-horse for not making greater haste; for he had learned from the waiter, who had, after due years of study and application, really mastered "Bradshaw," that there was a train just starting for the north.

"Push along, there's a good fellow! If you're in time you shall have an extra shilling."

Down came the storm of lashes—pitilessly— on the poor brute, who made a sudden exertion, leaped forward, and, being at the time utterly worn out, fell, and caused the Lieutenant's knees and toes to suffer, by the crash of the portmanteau against them, a little of that thing which he was so ready to inflict—pain.

We should not like faithfully to depict the Lieutenant's language and state of mind at this new infliction on his temper. It was not only the delay and the bodily anguish (for one corn on one particular toe was in a violent state of inflammation before this new injury to it), but also the jeers and comments of the bystanders that he had to bear.

However, the Lieutenant got out, gave the man a shilling as he stood staring sulkily at his horse, snatched forth his portmanteau, took another cab, and was soon at the station.

"In time?" he shouted to the porter.

"I'm afraid not, Sir. Be quick."

"Come along, then," said the Lieutenant to the porter, who shouldered the portmanteau and ran after him. The Lieutenant had got no ticket, but he determined to fight that question if any obstacle were interposed. And as he was starting from head-quarters they couldn't charge him too much at the other end.

He got on to the platform, saw the train moving, made a kind of desperate rush at it, but was stopped by the officials.

"Too late, Sir!" and as he stood there, baffled and gnashing his teeth in vexation, thinking that the detective himself might be in that very train, and so might have been stopped if only he could have been spoken to, who should he see but the great man himself, Mr. Smart, putting his head out of the window of a carriage, and waving his hand, as if to bid him be of good cheer, and to suggest he should be sure to bring him back his long-lost son.

He went to the refreshment-room to wait for the next train in two hours, and there drank half a bottle of wine before he had quite resigned himself to what now seemed, in all probability, inevitable—the detective's not only satisfying himself of the identity of Gent Rube with Rube, but of his participation in the robbery on the Squire's house.

He got away at last, and as he leaned back in the luxurious first-class carriage, and amused himself with a cigar in spite of the regulations, looking so fiercely as he lighted it at his only fellow-passenger, a nervous, youthful invalid, that the latter did not dare to remonstrate : as he thus made himself comfortable, he said to himself,

"Well, if I *can* find him anywhere on the road, or about the end of our journey, I *will;* if not, I must keep quiet at the Squire's, and be on the watch to make the best of things.

"But what about the Squire ?   What must I

tell him ?   If I say I have had no success, and then if he should by any chance get hold of this estimable and clever London friend of mine—by Jove! that would be awkward! Shouldn't wonder if he didn't run back from the seven thousand pounds, and leave me as bare as a plucked pigeon !

"But if I tell him everything just as it is, there's not only an end to the estates, but there's no saying how he may hamper me about this miserable lad.

" I think I'll see what my wife says first. She knows so much now that she may as well know all. I shall learn, at all events, from her whatever can be said on the Squire's side of the subject, without committing myself by first telling the Squire. On the whole, I think that's the safest."

Here the Lieutenant threw away the end of his cigar, and said to his companion,

" Like smoking ?"

" Well, not much, in a close carriage."

" Sorry. I'm going to have a nap now, and won't bother you again till I wake in an hour or two."

The invalid smiled and bowed, and presently the Lieutenant gave a great yawn, and then went off into a tolerably comfortable sleep, during which the invalid studied his face and amused himself by speculations on the character and position of this very easy-minded, cool, gentlemanly traveller.

"I ran it rather too close," said Mr. Smart, laughing to himself, as he saw the Lieutenant burst out upon the platform in his great hurry. "Wrong. I ought to have secured my train before he got my letter. I must mind better another time. It is evident he came flying as fast as he could to stop me.

"What does it mean? Can anything I said have convinced him beyond all question that Rube is Gent Rube? And is he so disgusted by the discovery that he doesn't even want me to know it? Or is there something more awkward still? Was he, I wonder, able at once to identify by his own knowledge Gent Rube with the robber of his own uncle? He looked strange when I told him about that; and yet he tried hard to seem as if he wasn't looking at anything or thinking about anything when I spoke.

"Well, now, here I am rattling along thirty-five miles an hour, and probably with him after me by the next train. He naturally guesses I should take this direction, though he can have no suspicion of my great discovery, through

Swell Jack, of the precise house in which the lad was a few weeks ago.

" This won't do. I can't have him hanging at my tail everywhere I go, or dodging me about, No. When I reach Rugby I'll make him think I have gone in quite a different direction to that in which his uncle lives."

So mused the detective, as he sat in the corner of a second-class carriage, with his comfortable travelling-cap drawn low over his forehead, so that the peak shadowed his face, while enabling him to look with his usual penetrating carefulness on his fellow-travellers.

At Rugby, he got out with his little bag in his hand, and walked up and down the platform, asking the porters, one after another, how he could best get to some town or village that nobody knew of in Lincolnshire; and at last, expressing his determination to go to Lincoln itself by the earliest train that would help him on his way.

Having thus made the porters who were hanging about particularly well acquainted with his person and supposed destination, he let the train go off that ought to have taken him on, and went to the refreshment-room and sat down to write a letter, which ran thus :—

" Dear Sir,—I am quite grieved we missed in

London at the starting of the train. Pity you could not have been half a minute earlier if you wanted me. I shall stop here at Rugby as long as I can, with the intention to see if you come by the next train before my own train towards Lincolnshire goes away. But as I do not suppose you were in such a hurry on my account, I shall not lose my train if I find one goes before you come, although I should have liked to be sure about your wishes now that I have seen you. I do not want to tell you yet of my plans, as they may fail; but I have a notion that a day or two in Lincolnshire will settle everything. I shall write to you from there or from London on my return, if I do not come to seek you in person at the close of my inquiries. If this reaches you on the platform here, please to give the bearer half-a-crown.   " Respectfully,

" C. SMART."

Mr. Smart read and re-read this with extreme deliberation before he put it in an envelope and addressed it—" Lieutenant Polwarth, Morley's Hotel, London."

He then went to one of the shrewdest-looking of the porters, and said,

" I particularly want this letter to be delivered to the gentleman to whom it is addressed, if he should come by the next train from London. He

will be in a first-class carriage, a haughty, aristocratic-looking gentleman, about forty or forty-
five, with a black, elegant moustache, and probably wearing a very light summer overcoat, with
velvet collar of the same colour. You can't miss
him if he comes, for you can soon run through the
first-class carriages, and ask every gentleman who
looks like him."

"I'll find him, Sir, if he be there."

"Very good ; if you do you'll get half-a-crown
from him. If you don't, then put the letter in
the post."

"All right, Sir."

"And now take my bag and get me a comfortable seat in a second-class carriage to Lincoln.
Look out for me on the platform."

"All right, Sir." And the porter pocketed the
letter, and took up the bag, while Mr. Smart
regaled himself with a piece of pork pie and a
pint bottle of pale ale."

Five minutes later Mr. Smart got into the carriage, but, strange to say for so business-like a
man, forgot his ticket. So the porter had to fetch
him one. And when he brought it and put it into
Mr. Smart's hand he found there a shilling,
which he smuggled into his own pocket with
entire satisfaction.

"You won't forget the letter ? "

"All right, Sir; if he comes he'll be sure to have it."

The train presently went off with Mr. Smart, and in due time the other train came, and the porter ran up to make his examination and inquiry. He was spared trouble, for he saw the handsome but disdainful face he expected—the moustache, and the light overcoat with the light velvet collar, bending out of the window, and calling,

"Porter!"

"Yes, Sir."

"Run for a shilling's-worth of cigars, and keep the change." So saying the Lieutenant put a two-shilling piece into the man's hand. And then, as the pale invalid heard, and got out in order to change carriages, the Lieutenant laughed, and said,

"Very much obliged; and really sorry to inconvenience you. But if I go I shall get where there are more people, and have less chance than here."

"Oh, I don't mind," said the invalid; and so they parted.

"Please, Sir, is your name Lieutenant Polwarth?" the porter asked.

"It is; but what the devil's that to you?"

"Letter, Sir;" and the porter handed it up, while he ran off to fetch the cigars.

"Letter! Who the —— corresponds with me in this fashion? Mr. Smart again, by Jove! So he's not going to my uncle's neighbourhood after all. Oh, very well; then he may inquire away as long as he likes. But stop! You never know how to have hold of these fellows. Don't let me make too sure this isn't a feint, and made because he saw me at the station, and thinks I may be following him."

The porter now returned, and a brief dialogue took place:

"Who gave you this?"

"Don't know—a respectable-looking person."

"What became of him?"

"Went off by the Lincoln train."

"Did you see him go?"

"I got his ticket for him and saw him off."

"Ticket to Lincoln?"

"Yes, Sir."

"All right. Here's eighteenpence more, making the half-a-crown you were promised, I suppose?"

"Yes," said the porter, and not with all the gratitude in his face that might have been expected at the gentleman's "dodge" to make up the half-crown. And as the Lieutenant went off he moralised to himself on the ingratitude of the unwashed class.

When it was quite night, a train from Lincoln set down many passengers, and among them a man with large red whiskers forming almost a beard, who happened to speak to this very same porter, in a loud, somewhat overbearing voice, to take his bag to the down train to the North. The porter got from him another sixpence, but he did not get from him what the man's love of fun strongly prompted, to say nothing of his desire for the information—a question of this kind that was framed within the lips, but did not get outside them,

" *Did you deliver my letter ?* "

A few hours later the Carslake coach put down this traveller in the close neighbourhood of the residence of Mr. Thomas Jessop.

"Ay, there it is—'The Traveller's Joy.' I wonder whether they met here—Gent Rube and Nobby Bob—the day of the robbery?

" What shall I ask for ? It's rather late to go to bed—nine o'clock; but if I don't it'll seem odd that I don't go on and finish my journey at once. I must have a night here, so I'll begin by having a good sleep through the day."

When he reached the inn he was too early for

Mr. Thomas Jessop, though he heard a ponderous step and an equally ponderous voice somewhere above; but there was the good-looking, black-eyed, and merry-voiced Mrs. Jessop, preparing her husband's breakfast, and who curtsied and smiled, and said, as he came in,

"Good-morning, Sir!"

"Good-morning! I have been travelling all night from London, and am going to Northope, to a Mrs. Maxfield ——"

"Oh, indeed! Very nice lady."

"But I am so thoroughly knocked up that I want to go to bed for a few hours."

"To be sure, Sir. Wouldn't you like some breakfast first?"

"No, thank you, for then I should not be able to sleep. Besides, I had some very early, while waiting for the coach."

"The bed's ready, and thoroughly well aired." So saying Mrs. Jessop led the way up an exceedingly narrow staircase, that made the visitor wonder what the giant would do if he were obliged to ascend it; and then into a fresh little room, with an old-fashioned heavy four-poster, with snow-white dimity curtains, and just room to stand at its foot between it and the dressing-table at the window, which opened on a very picturesque landscape.

"How clean and nice everything is here," said Mr. Smart, admiringly.

"You don't live in the country, I suppose?" said the little woman.

"No: but if I did I don't think I should always find so pleasant a place as this, or so agreeable a landlady. Eh?"

Mrs. Jessop coloured slightly, but began to move promptly off, saying, as she went,

"Shall I call you?"

"No; let me sleep as long as I can, for I am so dreadfully tired. Pray, is that your husband whose voice I hear?"

"Yes, and he wants his breakfast." And then she would stay no longer questioning, but disappeared.

"Now I wonder whether husband or wife will be the most communicative? Decidedly I know which would be most agreeable to deal with. Really I think I must marry, myself, some day. So, now for a good sleep before I see what mettle Mr. Jessop is made of, in that big body of his. How the house shakes as he goes!"

Five minutes later the detective was snugly wrapped within the sheets, and nothing could be seen of him but a little bit of white night-cap, of a rounded shape, that somehow emerged

from the bed on to the pillow, suggesting
anything rather than the scheming, worldly,
busy brain that was there, for a time, lying
quiet beneath.

CHAPTER XVI.

WHEN the detective awoke, he found himself sweltering with the heat of a summer afternoon, and with the whole force of the direct rays of the sun streaming in with a most inconvenient splendour. A great fly of some kind had come in through the partially open window and been caught within the meshes of a short muslin blind, and was buzzing away in immense dissatisfaction.

"What time is it, I wonder?" said the detective to himself, as he pushed the nightcap off his forehead, and rose on one arm to take his watch from the pocket above him. "Three, actually! and I came to bed before ten. Let me see. What'll be the right time to go down-stairs? Why, just too late to set off on a walking journey to Northope? If they're good Christians, they couldn't expect me to walk the distance in a leisurely manner in less than four hours. And, of course, they wouldn't expect me to get there in the dark. Three o'clock; two hours more, that'll be five; an hour for tea, six; and four hours' walk, ten: dangerous hour for unknown roads. Not to be thought of! The future Mrs. Smart wouldn't permit it if she knew, so I shan't. I shall turn, and, as the man in the play said, ' address myself once more to a snooze : ' not the exact words, I fancy, but near enough. Hallo! Who's that ? "

Mr. Smart's exclamation was produced by his hearing the sounds of a horse's feet, that had been clattering along the road, suddenly stop opposite " The Traveller's Joy," and a voice call out in loud tones, that he thought he knew,

" Well, Mr. Jessop, how do you do this fine afternoon ? "

" Pretty well, Sir, thank you," shouted out Mr. Jessop from his seat within the house. " Glad to see you back again."

" Any strangers here ? "

" Aha!" murmured Mr. Smart to himself.

" Only a gentleman going to Northope."

There was a pause, and then the speaker continued,

" Nobody asking for me, then ? "

" No, Sir."

" Good-morning ! "

"Good-morning, Sir!" And away the horseman rode, as if entirely satisfied. But Mr. Smart made no such mistake. His prompt inward comment was,

"Fairly caught, he thinks no doubt to himself. Of course he couldn't ask any more questions, for how did he know but I might be listening. He'll be back again soon, I'll bet a guinea to a sixpence, and most likely without his horse. I must get up and do or say something before he comes."

The detective began rapidly to dress, and was all the time silent and self-engrossed. Presently he opened the door and moved quietly down stairs, and then, opening another door, found himself in the august presence of the giant landlord.

At any other time he would have been greatly interested in studying the manners, mind, and character of this colossal specimen of the human race, who was content to let his greatness blossom in the desert air of the country instead of reaping a large income of wonder and money by public exhibition. But just now he could only think of the work in hand.

"The landlord, Mr. Jessop, I presume?" said he, with his most ingratiating manner.

"Yes, Sir, that's my name, and I'm not ashamed of it."

"If all I hear be true, it's a name rather to be proud of, I think."

The landlord looked at Mr. Smart as if in doubt of the sincerity of the remark, but seeing nothing in the stranger's face to contradict the respectful tone and sense of his words, he blushed like a girl, and said no more.

"I've had quite a long sleep, I find!" continued Mr. Smart.

"Yes, so the missus tells me," responded Mr. Jessop. "Good thing, sleep, when you need it. Come a long way, perhaps?"

"Yes; from Manchester yesterday morning, at London in the evening, and now here in the early morning."

"In the wool trade, perhaps?"

"The very thing!" said Mr. Smart to himself, "better than what I was going to say." Then he observed aloud, "Yes, I go hunting about now and then to open fresh sources of supply, and I've come here to see if a lady of the name of Maxfield, who, I am told, owns a great number of sheep at Northope, is inclined for business."

"Nice lady, but I don't think she changes much. She sells her wool to a man at Radford."

"Well, I can but try, you know. 'None but the brave deserve the *wool*,' we'll say;" and Mr.

Smart laughed and the landlord laughed too, and began rather to like his guest.

Just then the sound of a horse's feet was again heard on the road, advancing towards "The Traveller's Joy."

"I came down before washing my face," said Mr. Smart, "to see if Mrs. Jessop would be getting me a cup of tea ready, as I have a long journey before me, if I start to-day."

"To be sure. Here Missus!" shouted the landlord as the detective went out at one door and up the stairs, just half a minute before Lieutenant Polwarth came in at another, leaving his horse in the charge of a man outside, and calling out, in a loud voice,

"I can't find the gentleman I expected; he promised me to be at the hall about this hour, and I thought I would meet him. If you'll permit me, I'll sit down for a few minutes. No, no; never mind calling anybody, I can help myself to a chair. I'm told your ale is particularly good, Mr. Jessop. Well, if you do call, let Molly bring me a glass of that."

Molly brought the ale, and the Lieutenant for the first time sat down in Mr. Jessop's house and presence to drink it. The landlord, though wondering at the unusual condescension, felt a little pleased at the way in which it was done; and

the Lieutenant, while secretly disgusted with the
necessity imposed upon him, was rather proud of
his diplomatic skill, which might one day, he
thought, be of value to the country if he should
get the estates, get into Parliament, and—but we
need not at present follow his ambitious dreams.

"Capital ale!" he exclaimed as he set down
the glass, after drinking the whole off at once;
I must have another." Molly was called, and
replenished his glass. "Your visitor to Northope gone?" he continued.

"No; he'll be down directly to his tea."

"What's his business in this part of the
country?"

"He's a wool-buyer, from Manchester."

"Not a man with a scar on his cheek and a
black beard?" said the Lieutenant, making a
desperate plunge into the business of imaginary
personal description, that might be the means of
calling forth something not at all imaginary.

"Oh dear no; a face smooth enough and common enough, but with great red whiskers. Seems
an entertaining sort of man, quite free and easy.
Perhaps you would like to have a chat with
him?"

"Not the least desire in the world, Mr. Jessop," said the Lieutenant, rising, and paying for
his ale. "I don't think I care to wait. If any

gentleman wanting me should drive up to the door, you will, of course, direct him the nearest way. Don't send him round by the grand lodge. Good morning, Mr. Jessop."

"Good morning, Sir!" said the landlord, rising with immense effort, and looking quite purple with the effects of the sudden movement.

And again, as if the detective had been listening and enjoyed the fun of the thing, just as the Lieutenant went out he re-entered, saying,

"I thought I heard a gentleman's voice here, and I hurried down."

"Yes—gentleman from the Hall—Lieutenant Polwarth—expecting a friend."

" And the friend isn't come? "

" No, it appears not," said Mr. Jessop.

" Then suppose we have our tea? " added the stranger. " With all my heart," responded the landlord, thinking the stranger meant they should have it together. And Mr. Smart, though he had not meant anything of the thing, chuckled at this fresh bit of good luck. Now, at least, he would be able, he thought, to make good use of his stay at " The Traveller's Joy."

CHAPTER XVII.

"Won't Mrs. Jessop join us?" said the detective, as he gazed with a particularly satisfied expression of face on the contents of the table now before them. There were hot Yorkshire cakes, plain and with currants; hot buttered toast; delicious brown bread and butter, cut in the thinnest of slices; marmalade, raspberry jam, and several varieties of little biscuits. In the centre was a majestic old china teapot, pouring forth from its spout a steam of delicate fragrance. The detective was fond of good things, and, being blessed with a good digestion, and being accustomed to an open-air life, was able to do with a considerable share of them without much injury as yet to his constitution. But naturally he thought the unseen goddess who dispensed from her sanctuary called the kitchen all these delicacies ought to be herself a sharer in their enjoyment. Besides, he had other thoughts, which he did not care to speak of. He was greatly struck with her pretty, bright face, and held there could be no harm in having a good look at her in her husband's guarding presence. He knew also how much easier it was to set a lady's tongue going than a gentleman's; and, on the whole, he fancied he would succeed better in his object if he had man and wife to gossip with than one of them only.

"Nay, she cannot be persuaded," said the landlord.

"But, it seems to me positively shocking for two of us to sit down to such a table as this, with all these delicious provisions. Why, there's enough for half a dozen people."

"You see, it's the way of the women. They like, poor things, to see the men enjoy themselves, and don't mind so much for themselves."

"Comfortable theory for us," observed Mr. Smart, with a laugh.

"Not married?"

"No."

"I thought not, else you wouldn't have made such a remark—which, however, is quite true; but what's the use of dwelling on it, if the wife will have it so? My little woman—God bless her!—is a terrible despot in that way. It's no use trying to oppose her. So I resign myself to the idea that I must do my very best for my own enjoyment for her sake."

The two men both had a good laugh at this. But Mr. Jessop, after all, seemed to be struck by the observation, for he said, presently,

"We'll have the missus in. But then it must be for you. She won't come else. She never will. That's the one thing in which she disobeys. Here, Molly!"

Molly came.

"Molly, my wench, tell the missus that the gentleman would be glad if she would join us at tea, as he's a stranger in these parts—mind that, he's a stranger in these parts." As Molly went, he added, "Only appeal to her feelings, and you may do anything with that woman—I mean that's right and lawful."

The two men could hear through the open door towards the kitchen a whispered conversation.

"No, no; I can't. I've got these cakes to toast."

"I'll do 'em nicely, Missus."

"But I ain't clean."

"Lor, Missus!"

"There, don't gape at me like that; I mean I must put on a fresh cap, and another gown."

"I'll fetch 'em, and my little glass."

"Drat the men—make haste!"

Of course neither Mr. Jessop nor Mr. Smart appeared to hear any of this; on the contrary, they both continued their own conversation while the whispering in the kitchen was going on.

It was not long before Mrs. Jessop appeared with two more plates full of hot currant cakes in her hands, and her cheeks rosy with excitement. Mr. Smart jumped up, and placed his own chair for her, and fetched another for himself, and managed—sly rogue—so to seat himself and her that, while they all three seemed to be trying to face the open door in order to look out upon the pretty country, seen through it as in a frame, he could steal many a glance at the fair landlady without being detected by the husband.

After a few remarks, sounding unimportant, but which were so skilfully aimed at both husband and wife as to make them feel not merely at their ease, but in a particularly good humour with their guest, he thought to himself it was time to draw closer to the work in hand, while he was still unable to see how he could get them to talk about the one subject of all his anxiety, Gent Rube, without making them aware he wanted information.

Up to this moment nothing had been said that had the remotest connection with such a topic, and he was wondering whether he should be obliged to make a venturous plunge into it himself, without regard to inconvenient consequences; or whether he should still go on with general gossip, watching for some link that he might seize hold of to connect the talk with his secret aims, when the landlady unwittingly came to his relief.

"You won't go all the way to Northope to-night, will you?"

"I was thinking of it," said he, in a dubious tone.

"There's a half-way house, which you might reach before dark; a very good house, too."

"Better than this?" asked Mr. Smart, with an arch smile.

"Well, I'm not going to say anything about that," said Mrs. Jessop.

"But I am," returned the detective. "If I can't go right on to Northope to-night, I shall certainly be wise enough to know when I'm well off, and stay here—unless, indeed, you want to get rid of me."

"Oh! we shall be very glad of your stay; only ——" and there Mrs. Jessop stopped.

"Only my silly little wife doesn't understand the first law of business—look to your own interests only, and never mind your neighbour's."

"But is Northope too far to go to-night?"

" Why, it's a stiffish walk, and it's a lonely sort of way, part of the road," said the landlord.

" But no danger, I suppose ? "

" Not a bit."

" No robberies ever heard of here ? "

The landlord looked at his little wife, and she looked at him, and both looked uncomfortably on the ground. Ichabod ! The glory of a good character, they knew, had departed from the neighbourhood. They couldn't deceive anybody. Mr. Jessop wished now he hadn't said those last words with quite such a bounceable tone. He hemmed and his wife coughed. Then again he hemmed, with a more decided tendency towards speech, and the black sparkling eyes looked up full of confidence—it was all going to be explained by her husband—wonderful man !—whom nothing could put out.

" Well, you see," began Mr. Jessop, in an apologetic tone of voice, " we did have one or two unpleasant affairs a little while ago ; and when you put it to us about your going to Northope, we are bound to tell you the truth. I don't think there's a honester population anywhere than about here. I know anybody could rob me if they tried ; but I never was robbed— and, what's more, know I never shall be robbed, except by men foreign to these parts. And I mean to keep my eye pretty close on them if they comes in my way."

In his determination to watch such gentry the good landlord looked so sternly at the guest, that the latter said, with a laugh,

"I hope you don't suspect me."

The landlord looked at him for a moment, remembered what he had done, and burst into a great roar, which caused him to shake his chair —the room—the whole house, and Mrs. Jessop joined in with her silvery, merry laughter: both were evidently tickled with the joke of suspecting him, the good-humoured, respectable guest! As if he could have any act or part in the doings of such gentry!

As soon as the giant's mirth had subsided, and while wiping away the tears from his eyes, he related the stories (already known to our readers) of the robberies of the Squire and Mrs. Maxfield.

"Worst of all," said Mrs. Jessop, "the man was here that did the robberies."

"Yes," said Mr. Jessop; "but how could we help that?"

"Of course not," said the detective, who was wondering how he could get them to talk of what he did not know rather than of what he did. "The coachman told me all about that affair. It seems to have quite excited the neighbour-

hood. He said something about its being supposed there were more robbers in the business than the one who was killed."

"Yes; there was a servant, who ran away."

"Yes; and there was a young gentleman,"
interposed Mrs. Jessop, who repented of her
precipitancy as she saw a cloud darken the face
of her bulky lord.

"My wife means to say there was a young
fellow here, quite by accident."

"You mean he met the robber here quite by
accident on the very day of the robberies?"

"Yes," said Mr. Jessop, though not exactly
approving of his own meaning when it came
through other lips. "But he had nothing whatever to do with the rogues."

"Who was he?"

"A tuner of pianos, or something of that
sort."

"Quite a stranger, then?"

"Yes."

"Of course it was proved he could have had no
hand in the business?"

"Oh, yes. He was examined at the inquest,
after he had shot the robber."

"How came he to go to the Maxfields to lodge
after they had been robbed?"

"Why, he came up with them just when they

had been robbed, and helped them, and was very useful."

"I see; and so went afterwards to the house, and was made welcome ? "

"Yes; and it was supposed he and the daughter were making it up together."

"Indeed!   Is she anything particular ? "

"Anything particular ? " echoed Mr. Jessop, with a bit of generous scorn flushing up his face. "She's the most beautiful girl in the whole valley; and she'll have all her mother is worth, and that's not a little."

"Yes ? " said Mr. Smart, as if waiting for the landlord to go on.

"Well, either it was all a mistake, or else some quarrel, or something or other, has happened, for he went away quite suddenly—just when people were getting used to him, and getting to like to do the widow's business through him; he was so clever and correct."

"And nobody knows why ? "

"No ! "

"But I suppose it was the old story—one would and one wouldn't.   Of course it was the lady who wouldn't, and not the gentleman ? "

"Little doubt of that, I reckon.   He wasn't a fool."

"But perhaps fortune hasn't favoured him personally ? "

"What say you, Missus ?   Don't be afraid.   I shan't be jealous."

"Well, we thought him an uncommonly handsome young gentleman," observed Mrs. Jessop.

"Mark the duplicity of the sex—we ! " added the landlord.

"Well, you know you said so too," exclaimed Mrs. Jessop, blushing the while, and giving her husband a little slap on his broad cheek, which he seemed to enjoy amazingly, and to be only too ready—in a Christian-like spirit—to provoke a similar treatment on the other.   And certainly the detective felt he would willingly change places with him.   But he went on :—

"A noticeable young fellow—so handsome, so brave, and so distinguished as the protector of the fair sex.   But he's gone, you say ? "

"Yes, and I'm sorry for it.   I did take a fancy to that young chap."

"What's he like, and what's his name.   I wander about a good deal, and might by chance come across him, and give him a word from you."

"His name's Reuben Polwarth."

Detectives never start, or certainly Mr. Smart would have started then to hear a name so unexpected, and which carried him at once so directly to the end of the discovery he desired to make. Reuben Polwarth! Of course, then, this was not only the Gent Rube of the thieves' quarter, but the son of the Lieutenant, whose very name he had already taken. What could that mean but that he knew of his parentage? All this darted through the detective's mind as he heard the words repeated by the landlord,

"Reuben Polwarth." Turning to a new-comer, he said,

"Well, Tommy Larke, how are you this evening?"

"Pretty well, maister. Pint o' yale, please."

Mr. Smart saw it was a stupid-looking youth in a smock frock who was thus addressed, and who sat down gaping with open mouth at the tea-table and the good things upon it, so he went on with the conversation, striving to keep it on Reuben.

"What made people think so unlikely a young fellow should have been an accomplice in a robbery?"

"I'll tell you," whispered Mr. Jessop, bending low his head. "Because we've got fools and busybodies here, just as you have, no doubt, where you live. That fellow there—that lout who has just come in—set going a tale that he had seen the two gentlemen together before they appeared separately at my house."

"I see. Of course, if true, a very suspicious circumstance."

"But it wasn't true."

"Of course not; that's obvious. And how was it found not to be true?"

"Why, Tommy Larke swore he saw the young gentleman and, another older one walking together, and he identified the younger with Reuben Polwarth, but he couldn't identify the elder with the man who then lay dead in the yard."

"No," said Mrs. Jessop; "not even though the Coroner told him that the dead man, who then looked like a carpenter, had worn black clothes the day of the robbery, and had had a deal of hair, just as Tommy described." Here the landlord broke in,—

"Tommy couldn't have mistaken the robber if he had seen him, for he had such short, disgusting-looking arms; besides, that man, when he came in here, carried a bag, and Tommy was certain the gentleman in black he saw with the young gentleman had not got a bag." Mr. Smart shook his head and said,

"If that was all I shouldn't make much of that. He might have put the contents of the bag in his pocket, and concealed the bag itself under his clothes; such fellows don't care to let anybody see how they carry their tools."

Mr. Jessop and his wife both seemed to feel that the stranger spoke very sensibly; and, somehow, the former felt his own old suspicions reviving in an uncomfortable kind of way. He didn't for a moment believe the young fellow had had anything to do with the robbery, but he saw clearer than he had before seen the fact, how easily a stranger might be led to draw different conclusions; so he began to speak with a generous earnestness,

"If you had seen that young fellow as I did— not only here on the day of the robbery, but afterwards at the inquest—you would say as I did, 'That lad was never made to be a thief!' I said so then, and I say so now."

"I can assure you that all you tell me gives me quite an interest in him. I should very much like to see him and shake hands with him. Upon my soul I should."

"Good evening, John!" said the landlord to a new-comer.

"Good evening, Mr. Jessop!"

"I have been telling this gentleman all about our great robbery; but I left you to tell your share in it."

This was exactly what John Plackett liked, who soon began and narrated, with marvellous minuteness of detail, all his adventures ; and the landlord smiled as he listened and noticed how the story increased in vividness of colour and grandeur of proportion at every fresh recital. Mr. Smart listened, and drew from it just the one fact he desired to know, that Lieutenant Polwarth was perfectly well assured from his own experience, joined to his (the detective's) discoveries in London, that Gent Rube was the robber of his uncle's house, and therefore that *he* must think all further proof that Gent Rube was also his son as useless as it was disagreeable.

After learning everything that could be learned from "The Traveller's Joy," the detective seemed to get weary of the subject of the robbery, and he soon set the guests off upon other topics, and managed to interest them so much by his judicious behaviour, that after a little while every one had forgotten that Gent Rube and the burglar had at all engaged their attention, and were busily engaged in discoursing—somewhat uproariously—the mysteries of spirit-rapping and table-turning. Then Mr. Smart determined to withdraw, satisfied they would not, when he was gone, dream for a single moment of his true object.

So he said to Mrs. Jessop,

"Please to let me know what I have to pay, for I shall be off very early in the morning, and walk to the half-way house to breakfast."

She brought the slate; and the score—an exceedingly moderate one—ten pence for the tea, for instance—was at once paid, and he shook hands with Mr. Jessop, and then with Mrs. Jessop: and his warm pressure seemed to bring the colour to her cheek, but still she took it in good part as mere good feeling, so smiled, and they parted, he saying, at the last,

"I will let you know if I see anything of your young friend."

"Well," thought he, as he got to his rooms and prepared once more for bed, "That's all very satisfactory. Very satisfactory, indeed! What have I gained? Let me sum up. The Lieutenant is the person he represented himself; is very much frightened about my possible presence here; is satisfied I am not here: and is also determined, for very good reasons, to stop all further inquiry about his son, if only he can find me. Very good; he must get up by four to-morrow morning if he is now to find me.

" What else? Why I know under what name he is going, and that that is his own father's name. I know, therefore, that the Lieutenant's son and Gent Rube are, beyond all reasonable doubt, the same person; I know how to find a valuable witness if desired—this Tommy Larke, whom I should only like to have under cross-examination. Farther, I know he has left Northope unexpectedly, and I can guess why. He has been found out. The discovery does credit to the powers of the ladies. I mustn't forget the hint about the younger one. If it's a case of love, I begin to see the whole more and more clearly. The sight of her has given new zest to his wish to play the part of an honest man.

"Well, and if he does carry out his determination, why shouldn't the father take him back? By the Lord he shall, or pay me handsomely for not doing it. Business is always pleasant when it promises to be attended with profit; but when business and sentiment come together, the attractions are irresistible. The young fellow ought to be found; he shall be found, and, before long too, or I will confess myself no longer up to my work.

"Good-night, pretty Mrs. Jessop! I wish that big fellow would die by the time I'm ready to settle in the country. Good-night! Certainly yours are the finest black eyes I ever gazed on. Good-night, my bonny little woman!"

CHAPTER XVIII.

MR. SMART AS A WOOL-BUYER.

"How the deuce am I to play the part of a wool-buyer?" asked Mr. Smart of himself the next morning, as he trudged along down the sloping road of Northope. "I ought to have put myself under that bright youth Tommy Larke for a week's instruction into the qualities of sheep and wool. Would it help me even yet, if I were to catch hold of one of those fleecy animals that I see scampering about the hillside and cut off a handful of its coat to experiment upon? I fear not. Perhaps the widow doesn't want to change her present connection. I hope so; then I shall get on.

"This is the house that was described to me. I wonder if I look woolly enough in my face and dress to be taken at my own valuation?"

The detective gave a good rap at the door in the porch with his thick stick, but obtained no sort of answer. Again he knocked and louder, and at last the servant came, half undressed and in a great perspiration, fresh from the churning in which she was engaged.

"Does Mrs. Maxfield live here?"

"Yes; but she isn't at home."

"Not at home?" said the detective, with a sharp, suspicious glance at the girl, which, however, changed into a smile, as he remembered he was no longer in the neighbourhood of the police courts and of metropolitan habits.

"No. She's gone to see a neighbour that's poorly."

"Oh! Then she's not likely to be very long?"

"She may be an hour, may be two, before she get's back."

"I wanted to see if she had got any wool to sell this year. I'm told she is likely to have a good deal."

"Would you please to come in and wait?"

"Perhaps I had better. Is there no one else at home I could speak to?"

"There's the young lady. But she isn't very well, and she doesn't attend much to such things."

"Oh! indeed," said the detective, following the girl into the large parlour, with the great windows looking out on the lawn, and stream, and pine-clad moor beyond—a place by this time tolerably well known to our readers.

"Sorry to hear the young lady isn't well!" continued the detective.

"No; she isn't indeed!   And the doctor can't do her any good."

"Really!"

"She mopes, and don't eat; and she's almost always crying if you come upon her, promiscous-like, when she doesn't expect you."

"Though I haven't the pleasure of knowing the young lady, I am quite concerned at what you tell me. But I dare say you could guess now what's the matter, if you chose?"

The girl laughed, and then again turned grave.

"She's never been right since the man was shot in this very room."

"This room!" echoed the detective, as he gazed around with new interest.

"Yes, it was here; the robber came in at that window, between midnight and daybreak, and it was very dark, and the young gentleman stood just where I am now when he fired, and the young lady was outside, having just given him the things to load his gun with. And when she came in, and Missus and me after her, the robber was lying dead just there—you see the stains in the carpet—and the young gentleman looking almost as ghastly at what he had done as the robber himself looked."

" Shocking, shocking! No wonder your young mistress does feel it deeply that such a thing should have happened in her house."

" You see that little building there among the trees, just under that rocky part of the hill ? "

" Yes."

" The robber was buried there."

"Indeed ! "

A bell now rang and interrupted the gossip.

" It's Miss Bella ! She wants to know who it is, I dare say."

" Say a gentleman from Manchester, in the wool trade, would be glad of a few words with her, as her mother is out of the way."

" Yes, Sir," said the girl, as she hurried off.

" So," thought the detective, as his eyes continued to wander over the room, and the view from the window, and to that dark stain in the carpet, and then again through the window to the cemetery on the hillside, " it was here, then, poor Nobby Bob ended his career. What a place for a man like him to lie in ! One could fancy—only it isn't a Christian-like thought—that he was to be punished not only by his death for leading such a life, but that he was condemned, when dead, still to exist in a kind of eternal purgatory of peace."

The detective was interrupted by the appearance before him of a young woman of striking beauty, but of almost deathlike paleness. Mr. Smart hardly knew which most struck him, the exceeding loveliness or the exceeding pallor. But when she began to speak—and to a stranger—the sensitive blood, as usual, flowed to her cheek, and though it did not produce the old vividness of colour—for sorrow had left her no longer so open to impressions as she had been—still the detective understood at a glance how matters must have been for the youth he sought, who had been thrown into her society for weeks together, under circumstances calculated to make those weeks equal in effect to years of ordinary life.

She bowed, and took the chair which Mr. Smart at once offered her—as though he were the host and she the visitor—and when she sat he, of course, sat too, as he wished.

"Pardon my intrusion, but I don't know whether it is necessary for me to wait to see Mrs. Maxfield. I have understood she was likely to be making a change as regards the firm to which she generally sells her wool."

"Oh, no, Sir; we have a regular understanding with a gentleman at Radford, and I am quite sure he has done nothing to offend mother, for she had a kind letter and present from him only the other day."

" Oh, indeed! I didn't come here to interfere with other people's legitimate business, only if you had been going to change ——"

" If we had we should have been very glad," said Bella.

" But I will leave you my address, if you please, in case of accidents;" and Mr. Smart wrote on a little blank card, *Lamb & Co., Manchester*, and handed it to the young lady. " Lamb & Co.; we are well known on 'Change, though young in the business as yet."

" Thank you, Sir. Perhaps you would like a little refreshment?"

" Much obliged. I walked here from ' The Traveller's Joy ' this morning."

" Indeed!" said Miss Bella, with a slight though not unnoticed increase of interest in the tone of her voice. " And did you see Mr. Jessop?"

" Yes. Big man, isn't he?"

" Very," said Bella, with a faint smile.

" Doesn't often come to see you at Northope?"

" No; he hasn't been since ——" poor Bella was going to say " since the inquest," but she could not bear to finish the sentence, foreseeing instinctively the questions to which it might lead.

But Mr. Smart saw his advantage, and determined to press on. But she said,

"Excuse me for a moment," and went out.

"Shy—very shy! and miserable into the bargain. But, by Jove! she just is beautiful! It's nice to be brought up in Seven Dials and spend the flower of your youth in thieving, if this is to be the result—that I am to bring this young fellow back to take the Squire's estates at Wickham, and to marry this bit of pale loveliness. I shall begin to think honesty (in youth, at all events) isn't the best policy after all. She's coming back!"

The door was pushed open, and the servant entered with a heavy tray, which she placed before Mr. Smart, who, nothing loth, drew to the table, quite aware he could think, eat, and talk all uncommonly well together. Indeed he had a notion that he could at times use the eating process as a very safe kind of shield, behind which he could remain protected while himself peering out upon the enemy.

The tray contained the chief part of a cold fowl, accompanied by a piece of delicate pickled pork, also cheese, and a jug of ale, and bread, and biscuits, and marmalade. At the sight of all these good things, Mr. Smart began to feel his heart warm a little towards the beautiful but sad girl who had sent them to him, and he said to himself,

"She doesn't know the sort of price I am going to pay her for these little attentions, and I'm glad she doesn't."

Bella soon returned with an apology for her absence; and, though Mr. Smart was exceedingly polite, his way of beginning to evince his grati- . tude did not at all commend itself to her. After thanking her, and taking a few hearty mouthfuls and a prolonged draught, he said, as though the words had only just left her lips,

"You were saying, when I interrupted you, you had not seen Mr. Jessop since ———"

"Not since some business brought him here a few weeks ago."

Seeing this movement failed, Mr. Smart lost no time in originating another:

"I found him a most interesting companion while I stayed there yesterday."

"Yes," said Bella, in a tone of distant acquiescence.

"Among the many things I heard in relation to the neighbourhood, I was very much struck by the story of Mr. Reuben Polwarth."

Bella's pale cheek flushed into sudden colour,

but it was rather the emotion of anger than of shame. She said at once, in stern though agitated tones,

"I will tell my mother what you say. The servant shall show you out when you wish to go. Good morning!"

Most men would have been taken a little aback by this: not so Mr. Smart. To her astonishment, he addressed her suddenly in quite a different manner from what he had previously done, saying,

"Miss Maxfield, I beg you ten thousand pardons; but I have something particular to say to you which I have not yet said, and which will, I am sure, excuse to you my apparent rudeness."

He immediately went to her and took her hand in a manner at once so firm and yet so respectful that the poor girl, unused to men of the world, and only fearing or hoping—for she did both in a single second of time—she was going to hear something of Reuben, yielded to his request that she would again seat herself.

"In one word, then," he began, "I am about to repose a great confidence in you; and I trust, when you see my motives are good, that you will respect my confidence and not repeat to any one what I am about to say."

"You surprise me, Sir—so much—that ——"

"I ask no pledge. I only wish you to understand that, at present, I appear here as a buyer
of wool; and you must not, directly or indirectly,
interfere with that statement; for, if you do, you
will peril great interests that are intrusted to me,
and perhaps injure those towards whom"—
the detective hemmed and coughed, to give himself a little extra time for a proper finish to the
sentence—"towards whom, I doubt not, your
kind feelings and sympathies would flow if you
knew the whole truth."

"If I knew the whole truth!" repeated Bella
to herself; and Mr. Smart could see the beautiful lips quivering with the unspoken words.
"Does he mean that he is seeking Reuben—
perhaps to give him up to justice—and that he
wants my sympathies for the people he has in-
jured? Would to Heaven he would go, or let
me go! He can have nothing but fresh misery
to give to me."

"Miss Maxfield, I will tell you, what I have
most carefully guarded from every other person
in the neighbourhood: I seek Reuben Polwarth."

"And you look to me to find him for you?"
demanded Bella, now starting up, with such a
generous scorn upon her face as made even the
detective feel for the moment a little uncomfortable.

"I do," he said, with imperturbable good humour; "and I beg you to make no mistakes, but look on me as a friend."

"A friend!" echoed Bella, again wondering what the man could mean. If he were really aware of her secret feelings towards Reuben, and yet wanted her to help to discover him and give him up to justice, what did he—what could he —mean by talking of himself as a friend?

"Yes, Miss Maxfield, a true friend, if you take any kind of interest in the welfare of this unfortunate young gentleman. His whole future may now depend on your wisdom and kindness."

"Pray speak, Sir, fully, what you have to say. You make me only wonder more and more at every word."

"I will do so, and gladly, if I may only be sure that I shall not be injuring him or his prospects."

"What can his prospects be to me, Sir?" said Bella, again struggling with her indignation that any stranger should thus play with all her most sacred and most secret emotions.

"I grieve to hear the question. Perhaps I have been, then, altogether misled. I thought to find for him a friend ——"

"For him?" said Bella, in tremulous accents.

"Yes. May I now speak?"

Bella seemed to know all he meant, yet did not know what else she could do than bow silently, as if in acknowledgment that she did at least wish to know how she could help Reuben Polwarth in his need.

"I know not, Miss Maxfield, how far you are acquainted with this young gentleman's past history ——"

Bella noticed that phrase a second time—"young gentleman," and was strangely puzzled by it. The detective continued,

"But I shall probably convince you of my knowledge when I tell you his past has been one for which all his friends must blush or sigh."

Bella was silent. He could not see her face, for she had turned away, but he saw how she trembled at his words.

"But then he has great excuses, more I think than you can know of."

Bella listened intently, but said nothing.

"But *I* know that he was a gentleman's son, born with great expectations, but left to live in the deepest poverty and degradation on account of his mother's errors. She is now dead, and has been for some years, and it is only by an extraordinary combination of circumstances that the truth has become known to me. Do I weary you?"

"Oh, no! no! no!" said Bella, turning to him just for one moment, with streaming eyes and imploring look.

And then Mr. Smart sketched the broad outline of Reuben's story as told to him by the Lieutenant.

"What is his name ?—the gentleman's—Reuben's father ? " she asked in low tones.

"Everything but that; everything but that, my dear young lady, I will tell you! But you mustn't ask me for that—not at present, at least. I must not expose him. It is he who employs me."

"He!" wonderingly said Bella.

"Yes. He has no children by his second marriage; so he and his wife have made it all up about the first affair, and agreed to find the missing lad; and if he be found he will, unless the past stands in his way, be the heir to very large estates.

"Wonderful! Wonderful!" Bella murmured to herself. And she seemed to feel now that her own favourable impressions towards Reuben were in a measure explained. But a new thought made her say aloud, "Why do you fear the past stands in his way, if the father knows of the past and yet sends you to seek him ?"

" Come—come, young lady. I see you can be

acute enough. Your question is very much to the purpose, but I won't answer it. That's two things I won't tell you—the father's name, and why there is a doubt about the son getting the estates, even though I am sent to find him. But, positively, I will make no more reservations."

" And what do you look for from me ?"

" Only the means of finding Reuben Polwarth."

" I do not know where he is."

" Probably not; but I can make a deal of use of a very small fact, if only you will really help me to that extent."

Bella looked at the detective, and he looked at her, and there was a significant silence for, perhaps, half a minute.

Again she looked at him, and this time he not only smiled, but said,

" I know of what you're thinking."

Up went the vivid colour into Bella's cheek, but only for a moment; and she soon regained her self-possession, as she said, also smiling,

" Indeed ! "

" Yes. Tell me if I am right. You were saying, ' Gracious Heaven ! If this man tells me false ! If he is here only to get hold of Reuben and drag him to prison; and if I allow him to make me the instrument !' There, young lady; putting aside the exact words, wasn't that about it—the real thing?"

" I—I—perhaps—yes—but I fear no longer. You cannot be so base."

" Well, I am not particularly good. Don't rely too much on that. I come from a queerish place in respect to morality; but this you may take your affidavit upon — I am not the rogue to injure you or this young fellow, towards whom I am beginning to feel a personal liking, though I never saw him. So, come now—you know all. If you don't give me some hint at guidance, I shall have to go back and tell my employer I have failed. The poor lad must go his own way to perdition."

" Excuse me—you don't know—that——"

" Oh yes, I do! I have heard he has re-formed; and I don't wonder now—with such a motive."

Bella wanted to be angry, but could not manage it. There was a certain geniality in the stranger's brusque manner that gave her a liking for him now that she found in him a friend of Reuben.

" I will be back in a minute," said Bella, rising and stepping rapidly across the room to the door, and going away.

" Will it be best for me to wait for the mother,

after this ? " mused Mr. Smart to himself during her absence, which lasted but for a minute. At Bella's return, breathless through ascending and descending the stairs so rapidly, she said,

" I expect my mother back every minute, and I should like to leave you before she comes. Here is a letter we received from him inclosing some money." She put it into the detective's hand, who read as follows :—

" Madam,"

" It is addressed to my mother," interposed Bella.

" Madam—I do not send you the inclosed money as a kind of indignant reproof of your injustice to me at our parting; I send it to you because I felt I had no right to retain in my hands unnecessary articles of luxury, while the work of restitution was not even begun. I have sold my watch; I have retained from the pro-ceeds enough for my wants for some weeks, and I now dispose of the remainder in replacing small sums of money that have caused me special pain to reflect on, owing to their accompanying circumstances, and among these is the sum that was in Miss Maxfield's purse.

" I retain, and shall continue to retain to my

dying day, the portrait which you so unwillingly allowed me take away.

"REUBEN POLWARTH.

"CHESTER, *Sunday evening.*"

"And is that all you know of him?"

"That is all," said Bella, sadly, yet with a look that seemed to fancy she hoped he would extract more from it than she could. Presently she continued, "you see that Mr. Polwarth ——"

Bella was not able to go on.

"Yes; I see that he is what I thought, a true, though unfortunate gentleman, in soul as well as in blood, and we must do our best to set him in his proper place."

"My mother is coming up through the village. You will, of course, wait to see her?"

"Well, no; I have got all I want. Perhaps, in the interest of the young man, it may be as well to keep our own counsel for the present."

"Oh! but I cannot do that; it would be so ——"

"Yes, yes, I see. Tell her, then; but don't tell her the name of the father, or why the estates are not certain to go to him." The detective laughed. "You see I hadn't overlooked that you would want to tell all you were going to learn."

" Then you won't wait ? " said Bella, looking anxiously across from the side of the window where she could just see the village road, as if she didn't particularly want him to wait.

" Well, no ; if you are quite sure your mother has no wool to spare ! "

" Oh, yes," said Bella, unable to resist a smile, " I am quite sure of that."

" Very well, then, I take my leave, and shall hope. I have fared better than other wool-gatherers proverbially do fare in getting this clue —Chester. Good-morning ! " He put out his hand, and she allowed him to take hers, and to hold it, as she said, faintly,

" Good-morning ! " in a tone that implied to the experienced Mr. Smart that he had not said all to her she thought he ought to say, or hoped he would. He guessed the truth, and remarked, as if he had previously intended to do so,

" And, if I should hear anything, or want to know anything, may I presume so far as to write to you ? "

" To my mother, if you please ; I will take care you are answered."

" I understand."

They shook hands again, and Mr. Smart saw that that last bit of talk had more cheered the pale, fair girl than all the rest put together.

When he got outside he saw a lady—evidently Mrs. Maxfield—coming up towards him; but, though he looked her way, he did not seem to see her, and most provokingly turned in the other direction and walked so fast that she could not possibly stop him. However, she hurried in to learn who the visitor was—from Bella's lips— who could at least now speak without having a stranger's eyes fixed upon her during the narrative.

CHAPTER XIX.

"CHESTER!" mused the detective to himself as he entered that ancient city on a Sunday evening after service time, when the streets were full of well-dressed people, many of them going forth for a walk in the beautiful environs. " Chester ! There's an address now for a sensible young man to give ! Well, I must take my chance, as usual, and trust that my luck will help me."

He found a quiet inn where he could stay; and, having deposited his bag and made himself look a little less like a traveller, he set out again to amuse himself by wandering through the city, trusting that some incident or some thought would, sooner or later, suggest to him how to proceed the next morning.

He was greatly taken by the " rows "—those curious nests, or, rather, galleries of shops, which occupy the spaces in the houses that ordinarily form the first stories over ordinary shops, and to and from which you ascend and descend by flights of steps at intervals. But still he could not for an instant forget the business that had brought him hither, and he thought to himself,

"Reuben Polwarth may even now be within fifty yards of me—perhaps walking with one of those pretty girls I see moving so numerously about: Northope and Nobby Bob alike forgotten."

Then, having got on to the city wall just where one of its gateways crosses a principal street, he became interested in that new feature of the city; and, being told he could make the whole circuit of the city by keeping on the wall, and so get the best view of the former at the same time, he started on, past the tower whence Charles I. saw the destruction of his army on the neighbouring moor; past the primeval-looking cathedral, and its surrounding orchard and other grounds, down into which he looked from his height of vantage; past the racecourse and the gaol, the latter making him pause for a good long look, ending in the remark,

"Has he got in there, I wonder?"

Then the beauty of the Dee, and of the country on the other side, struck him; and he saw the handsome canopied boats lying below ready for pleasure-hunters, and he wondered if Reuben

Polwarth had already got comfortable enough to be enjoying himself that way. And so he got back to the place where his circuit had begun—the gateway over the street—and he was obliged to own he did not feel himself a bit wiser as to his future proceedings.

When he returned to the inn he had some tea and cold meat, naturally thinking, as he had probably hard work before him, he would prepare himself accordingly. And, as he enjoyed himself over this meal, he took up a local paper from the sideboard, and began to hunt through its columns as if reading only the short paragraphs and the advertisements, evidently still having in his mind the one predominant idea,

" How the d— am I to find this Reuben Polwarth ? "

The city paper proving as blank as the aspect of the city itself to illumine the detective's darkness, he went to bed—not much better personally, we fear, for the day, which he only remembered (as usual) to be Sunday by its compelling him in a measure to suspend operations.

However, after breakfast next morning, he determined, since he could not begin on a particularly brilliant plan that would be likely to carry him at once to his mark, he would, at all events, begin somehow, even if it were but by the exceedingly commonplace mode of asking the waiter if he could direct him to the man he wanted.

"Polwarth! Young man! Something to do with music! Never remember any such person stopping here; but I think there's a person of that description living down by the Baths," said the brisk waiter. "Yes, I do think his name is Polwarth, and that he is a tuner of pianos. Glass of sherry, Sir?" said he, suddenly, to another customer, and then was off.

Mr. Smart was soon at the Baths, and inquired there for his man. The name Polwarth was quite unknown. But was there no piano-forte tuner?

"Yes, there was;" and the house was indicated. Thither went Mr. Smart and saw in the window, among a collection of children's toys—some of them supposed to be musical—an accordion or two; and he read, on a label in a frame, "Palmer;" and he saw within a fat and frowsy-looking man of forty or so smoking his pipe and looking wistfully up into the cloud of smoke he was making, as if he saw there something much more worth thinking about or looking after than the place or the people about him.

"Of course," said the detective, "this is the waiter's notion of what I wanted. Very well. Perhaps he was right, though not exactly in the way he had intended." He went in.

"Do you happen to know a young fellow of the name of Reuben Polwarth?"

"No."

"I think he is a musician of some kind, or a tuner of pianos."

"Don't know him. Perhaps Johnson, No. 11, in that street down yonder, may. He is a tuner."

"Thank you, most likely he will."

Mr. Johnson's house was soon reached. The tuner was from home, on one of his tours through the neighbouring country. Did Mrs. Johnson know one Reuben Polwarth? No. Did she remember any young man who had lately come to Chester in her husband's vocation? For, perhaps, the querist might be mistaken in the name. Well, she said, there was a young man that had come to them not long ago.

"His name?" interrupted the detective.

"John Smith."

Now, precisely because John Smith is not a suggestive name, did it seem particularly to interest Mr. Smart. He became at once quiet but watchful and inquisitive.

"He wasn't worth much; for my part, I can't imagine where he learnt his business, he went about it so oddly."

"I have got him," thought the detective.

" But he didn't want much salary, and seemed so respectful like at first, and so willing to be told."

" Aha ! Master Reuben Polwarth ! " again said the detective to himself.

" But we took kindly to him, and then, one morning, what do you think he did ?—why, went off with my husband's watch and all my silver spoons."

The detective's face at this announcement did really change a little—not a very common circumstance with him. At first this seemed like proof that the culprit was not only the man he sought, but that he had relapsed, and into a baser degree of baseness than the detective could at all understand.

" What sort of looking young man was he ? "

" Nothing particular; but he had a large wen, or something of that kind, on his neck from a boy, which made him always hold his head a little on one side."

" Indeed ! " said the detective, with a smile, and beginning to recover his equanimity. " No moustache, I suppose ? "

" Well, my gals say he was trying hard to get one to grow all the while he was here, but it wasn't of much account."

"Thank you!   He is certainly not the person
I seek."

The detective felt now set loose to float about
on the stream of chance or circumstance, without sail, or oar, or anchor of any kind.   He went
to every inn in the town—to every lodging-house;
he got hold of every porter at the station; bribed
the letter-carriers to make inquiries for him;
went to the newspaper-offices, thinking Reuben
might be answering advertisements or himself
advertising; but these, and a variety of other
measures, all alike failed.

"Of course! of course!" communed he with
himself, in the bitterness and vexation of his
spirit; "I might have been sure of it. This
aimless and brainless kind of work never does
come to any useful end. It's a theory of mine
that, given a full knowledge of a man's position
and character, a true detective ought to be able
to tell what that man will do in any and every
contingency of life. If I were he, what should I
do? Let—me—see. Whenever two paths open
—one of which a humbly-born man would be apt
to tread, while the gentleman born would most
likely take the other—he, Reuben Polwarth, will
be sure to choose the gentleman's. But he has
no money—no friends—no recommendations.
Banks,   railways,   solicitors'   offices,   baths,

churches, races, tradesmen, workshops—thus I keep turning over all kinds of people and possibilities, but can see none likely to be useful to him. I saw some navvies at work near the railway; but he wouldn't be strong enough for that work, and he and his comrades would hardly suit; else good hard work offered, and no questions asked, would be tempting to Gent Rube, gentleman or no gentleman. And he might do something of the kind for a time to keep body and soul together.

"Or, he may have gone wandering about this city, glancing sidelong into people's faces, pausing at all sorts of shop-windows to measure the looks of the man within, and only at last making a venture when he saw a countenance or heard a voice that seemed to be a bit genial to him.

"I'll go out again with that very idea. I'll watch every face, haunt every shop, and always ask myself—'Is this the sort of person that he would have been likely to speak to?'"

The detective took up his hat, and started off once more to see if he could now learn anything of the fate of Reuben Polwarth by seeking a true philanthropist.

CHAPTER XX.

MR. SMART'S SEARCH FOR A PHILANTHROPIST.

IT was wonderful what a number of wants Mr. Smart suddenly began to discover he suffered from, and what great exertions he made to have them all satisfied. He wanted to ask questions about every old building he saw of every shopkeeper or resident in its neighbourhood; and, as such buildings are very numerous in Chester, that took up a deal of time. Then he wanted sundry small articles of wearing apparel, and, though he seemed in an uncommonly accommodating mood, still it was hard to please him by finding the exact thing he wanted. He wanted something to eat and drink incessantly, though it was odd enough he pocketed most of the edibles, and left after just tasting most of the drinkables. He wanted to know the price of this picture in one shop; the peculiarity of that saddle in another; the value of a new invention in lamps in a third.

While thus wandering about—seemingly moved
by no deeper feeling than a desire to amuse himself, but secretly scrutinising every face that
gave even the remotest prospect of the discovery
of such a person as he sought—he came, at different periods of the day, upon three individuals
with whom he trusted himself into closer inti-
macy. The first was a rosy-looking baker, a
man in whom the silvery-white hair seemed to
contradict the youthful bloom of his cheeks; and
who attracted the detective's attention by his
genial smiles and tones towards the children who
came in from time to time to buy cakes.

" Come, I'll have my first trial here," thought
the detective; so, having ordered a pound of
arrowroot biscuits to be weighed and put up, and
sent to his inn, he took a chair and began, after
a little preliminary gossip :—

" I suppose, Mr. Butter, you can't help me to
make a little discovery about which I am
anxious ? "

" I shall be delighted to try," said the rosy-
faced, silvery-haired baker, as he went on weigh-
ing the biscuits in his slow, impressive way.

" Well, there's a young fellow—a genteel-
looking chap he is when in his own proper garb
—who has been missed by his family, and it is
feared he is in difficulty. I want to find him,

and try if I can't make all smooth for him at home."

"Young, is he?   And a gentleman's son?"

"Yes."

They were interrupted by a woman and child who entered, both shabbily dressed, both looking as though they couldn't see any place in the shop humble enough for them to stand in while addressing its master; while the mother especially seemed to be in a nervous tremor as she was about to speak to him. But Mr. Butter did not wait for her to speak. His face became dark; all the oily sweetness disappeared from his voice; and when he opened his lips, it was like a clamorous east wind, both for loudness and bitterness, the breath that issued through them upon the half-starved woman and child:

"Now, ma'am, I don't want to hear any more talk; I want my money. If you can pay me, say so; if you can't, why then no more bread, and I shall put you in the Court to-morrow. That's my answer. There, go along!"

The woman and child obeyed, and went out in tears, shivering with the artificial cold of hunger, but not venturing to say another word.

"So, this is my philanthropist No. 1, is it?" thought the detective to himself. Then he said aloud, without another attempt to continue his story, "You needn't mind sending the biscuits to the inn, I'll take them, and there's the money."

"Much obliged; and as to this young gentleman——" But the worthy baker had happened to turn his eye to the shop window, and when he again glanced towards his customer he saw only the empty chair; the detective had gone.

Yes, the detective had gone, and, to his credit be it said, for once he could not resist the temptation to do a good act. He apologised to himself for it, as he moved rapidly after the woman and child, saying,

"I suppose philanthropy is one's natural atmosphere just now. Certainly I never felt so respectful an interest in that sort of thing before as I do to-day; and, though business is business in that as well as in everything else with me, I can't say it isn't business to dispose of some of my increasing superfluities before they accumulate to an inconvenient bulk."

On overtaking the woman he touched her arm, and said,

"I was in the baker's shop just now, and felt sorry to hear you so spoken to. Will you accept these biscuits for your child?"

The woman curtsied, looked scared, looked at her child, then, taking the bulky bag, burst into tears, and went away with a heartfelt,

" Thank you, Sir!   Oh, indeed, I thank you !"

In the face of this experience the detective could not, he felt, come suddenly to the conclusion that he was working on a false principle—the belief that there were philanthropists in the world, and, therefore, why not in Chester. But somehow the baker had made him very suspicious, and he determined, at all events, to mistrust in future rosy cheeks with silver hair and oily tones.

His second experiment was with a poor, miserable-looking chemist, who seemed to have so much need to feel for himself that the detective thought he might perhaps be the man whom he sought, as especially capable of feeling for others. There was something of the broken-down gentleman, something of the worn-out student, about the man that the detective fancied might arrest the anxious glance of Reuben Polwarth, if he had really once got into this shop while in great trouble.

It was the shop of all shops, too, for a young, desperate fellow to have chosen, if he had a mind to dispose of his difficulties by a dose of prussic acid. The detective found himself seriously hoping the young man hadn't been such a fool, and inclined to resent such an unbusiness-like termination to his—Mr. Smart's—zeal and ability.

But, on attempting to talk to him—he found him ready for any amount of listening—but not for the responsibility of knowing one single fact of all he had been told. Either the poor man's brain had become so hopelessly muddled that he didn't feel able to hold fast the thread of any discourse that didn't relate to his own immediate affairs, or sorrow had made him self-engrossed and, in a sense, unwilling to attend to any other person's miseries.

But he had not seen, or at least did not remember, any such person as Reuben ; and that was all that the detective could extract from his supposed philanthropist No. 2.

He was getting angry to be so ceaselessly baffled. He did not want to go back to Northope and say he had failed, and then try to extract from the Maxfields another glimpse of hope which might prove equally fallacious.

"No," he had said to himself. "This is become a matter of professional consequence. I *must* succeed !"

But how? He was determined to make one more experiment, and, if possible, that one should be so good, so well thought out, that it should lead him to triumph at last.

A happy thought struck him. He would go to that poor woman, and see if she could not direct him to some one who had befriended her, and who might have befriended others, and whose character might in some way have become known to Reuben Polwarth—if, indeed, he had been in this neighbourhood in a state of great distress. Of course, if he had gone from the place altogether before his means had failed, there was an end of the inquiry. Nothing more could, then, usefully be done at present.

He went straight to the baker, found him still in the shop, and not at all offended by the abrupt termination of the previous talk.

"Can you give me that woman's address who came to you with the child while I was sitting here? I merely want to ask her a question about the matter I was speaking of."

"To be sure. I will write it down for you. There it is. Good sort of woman, though troublesome. If you thought of helping her, your charity would be well bestowed."

"But I didn't."

"Oh! very well. If she or any friend would pay my little bill—fifteen shillings and sevenpence halfpenny — I wouldn't mind going on again for a time."

"I'll tell her."

"Or even if a part of it——"

"I'll tell her. Good-day!"

" Good-day. Deserving woman, I assure you."

The detective soon found the woman's house—a wretched sort of place—where, in a single room, he found her, her husband (who was lying on the bed ill), and four children.

She curtsied and smiled as he entered. It was but a faint smile, but somehow, it warmed Mr. Smart's heart a little as he felt its glow. She put a chair for him, and said, with a look towards the bed,

" My husband's been ill for more than five weeks, and he had been only partially employed before that; else we shouldn't have been so badly off as you saw."

" I came," said Mr. Smart, anxious to prevent painful mistakes, " merely to ask you about a young man, a young gentleman I might say, whom I am seeking. I fancy he must have been in great difficulty in this place as a stranger, and may have had to seek help from some rich or kindly-disposed person."

Husband and wife exchanged glances, and the former said, in a feeble though irritable voice,

" That there are such people here as well as in other parts I'm not going to dispute, but me and my wife haven't had the luck to know any of 'em. I came here seeking work five years ago, got it, pleased my employer, made friends among my neighbours, and things all went on well. But a bad time came, trade grew slack (I'm a carpenter by trade), and here we are—going, I suppose, into the workhouse, unless we prefer, as perhaps we shall, to die like dogs in our holes."

"No, no, John! I shall manage somehow, if you'll only keep quiet and get strong enough. Suffering frets him, Sir; he isn't used to sickness," said the woman, in an apologetic tone. Then she went on,

"What sort of person was this young gentleman you are looking for?"

"I can't tell how he might be dressed, or how he might look now or of late, but he was a very handsome young fellow, with a dark moustache."

Again the husband and wife exchanged looks, and Mr. Smart wondered what it meant, and began to watch.

"I seek him in behalf of friends who are most anxious for his return home; but I fear my difficulty in finding him is greatly increased by a special circumstance."

"And what may that be?" inquired the man, who seemed to get more and more interested, and who now raised himself upon one arm to look more closely at the visitor.

"Why, that particular thing which he knows and I know would make him disinclined to leave

any track behind by which he might be discovered."

Again the two exchanged looks, and there
came a long and inexplicable pause.

The woman looked inquiringly at the man, and
he nodded. She then said,

" What was your young friend's name ? "

" Reuben Polwarth."

" Then we know nothing about him. No."

" But suppose he did not tell you his true
name ? "

" He told us so much that I think he would
have told us that too," said the woman, who now,
to Mr. Smart's surprise, had tears in her eyes ;
not, apparently, about her own and her husband's
griefs, but in connection with some stranger,
whom she had for the moment supposed might
be the same the detective sought. The detective
repeated mentally to himself her words:—" He
told us so much," &c., and determined he would
not, at all events, leave the place till he knew
more about this " he."

Rapidly he ran through all kinds of possibilities connected with the notion that the
" he " was Reuben Polwarth. If so, why did she
seem to fear to talk about him ? Could he have
told them any part of his real story ? Was it
possible that these poor depressed creatures had

extracted from him confessions that the detective felt sure he would most jealously guard from all the world? Impossible! Yet what, then, made them so unwilling to speak? He must learn that. He must make a bold plunge.

"My good friends," said he, "I will, if you will permit me, place confidence in you for the sake of the man I seek. I will own to you that there is that in his past life which involves pain to reflect on—possibly danger—but which I and his friends wish now to guard him from. Is that your acquaintance? If so, pray speak, for his sake. Upon my soul you may do so. I am not related to him, but I am employed by his own father to find and take care of him for the future."

And there was a constrained and painful silence; but at last the man said,

"Well, Polly, I think you'd best tell the gentleman all we know, and perhaps he'll see it isn't the same man that we are talking about."

"Well, Sir," said the woman, "I think anybody who could injure that young gentleman must have a bad heart, indeed. And I'm sure you haven't, from your kindness to-day to me in the street.

"It was the day before my husband fell ill, and when he was coming home one evening late from his work in a village, that he come upon a young gentleman standing at four cross-roads, looking up at the decayed inscriptions and trying to read them.

"'What places are written here?' says he, 'I can't read them.' My husband told him, and then he thanked him; so pleasant and so sad that the master stared at him, and stopped and spoke a bit more, and by-and-by the young man he says, says he,

"'I suppose you don't know anybody who would give me a bed without being at all sure that I can pay them for it? Eh?'

"My husband laughed, and the young gentleman laughed, and then he would have gone away, but my husband said,

"'If you weren't joking, and really do want a bed, I think I and my missus could accommodate, if you won't mind what sort of bed it is. 'Mind!' said he, 'it's clean; but that's all I can promise!' 'Yes,' said the young gentleman; 'and you mind that, while I will pay you if I can, I tell you honestly that I am not sure about it; particularly if I leave the neighbourhood to-morrow morning.'

"'It's a bargain,' said the master; 'come along!' And he brought him home. And I never was so shocked when I saw by the light of the candle how thin and miserable he looked, for

all his handsome face; and then he was so pleasant, too, in his manner, when he spoke, as though
his pain and trouble didn't matter. And he began
to play with the children while I got him something to eat, and I don't believe he had eaten a
mouthful that day.

"Well, he stopped not only that night, but all
the next day and night, and somehow he liked
us, and said he had nowhere met such true
friends. Of course, we didn't take that for anything but his kind and grateful feeling, and we
began to wonder who and what he was like. And
at last we made sure he was a gentleman's son
under a cloud; perhaps he had done something
to give mortal offence at home, and was unable
to go back, or to get work, or to find any friends.
And we spoke to him. And then he told us his
whole story; how he had been brought up among
bad people in London, and had done wrong; and
broken off with his old companions in London;
but that go where he would, some one or other
of those men was sure to come across him and
upset him with his employers by revealing his
former condition.

"Poor young gentleman! he seemed almost
heartbroken as he let out to us that he did not
know really what to do next, or where to go.

"So we both tried to think what was best for

him—both my husband and I; and I remembered I had a brother about thirty miles from here, who might, if he would, employ him as a clerk, for he writes a beautiful hand; and I asked him if I should write and try. And he said, 'Please; but tell him what I have told you, for I am determined no longer to sail under false colours.' And we did, and my brother agreed to take him; though, as he said, he didn't like the idea of it; but, as the salary was low, he would try him."

"And did he?" broke in the detective.

"Yes," said the woman, wiping her eyes; "but I got this letter from him only two or three days ago."

She handed it to the detective, who read—

"ST. ASAPH.

"Dear Sister,—I am sorry to tell you your young friend has behaved very badly, and left me. I missed some money, and could find it nowhere. Wasn't it natural I should suspect him? I did, and told him so. I thought he would have gone out of his senses. But I stuck to my point till the money was found. Maggy, silly child, had taken it unknown to her mother and me; and then, of course, I was satisfied. But he made so much of the affair, that I was obliged to cut it short, and tell him to go about his business.—Your affectionate

"JABEZ STEVENS."

"And is that all you know?" eagerly asked the detective.

"No; only yesterday this came also by post." And the woman placed a scrap of paper in Mr. Smart's hand to read aloud. He did so, to the following effect:—

"Good-bye! God bless you both! I am obliged to wander again. It can't be for long. I shall never forget your kindness.

"REUBEN JESSOP."

"Jessop!" mused the detective to himself. "Jessop! Yes, I see. Compelled to change his name in order finally to break connection with the Northope doings, he has selected the name of the big landlord, who was evidently smitten with him. Well, I know not whether I have now finally found or finally lost my man. But this is him, beyond all question. And here, then among these poor creatures, after all, are my philanthropists, No. 3." And then he said aloud,

"I am glad to tell you we are all interested in the same person."

"Dear! dear! you don't really say so?" exclaimed the woman.

"Well, that is strange!" said the man.

"But quite true," added the detective; "and I shall be off either to-night or to-morrow morning to your brother to see if he can give me any hint for following him. The information you have given me ought to be paid for"——

Here he was interrupted by both husband and wife,—

"No—we don't wish anything of the kind."

"Well, then, take this sovereign to pay off that abominable baker, and as a bit of friendly help from me. Though, mind, I shall put it down in my employer's bill."

And they all laughed, and soon after parted.

CHAPTER XXI.

ON THE ROAD.

I⊤ is night; and the solitary traveller who is moving on, strangely absorbed, can yet note how wild and picturesque the country about him is growing. Higher and higher on each side of him rise, like black walls, the hills, with solitary lights sparkling here and there, suggesting to the despairing eyes that gaze yearningly towards them the bright firesides and comfortable homes within, whilst he—but there the thought is checked as with a sudden and half frenzied grasp —and the wanderer goes on.

On, still on, through the villages, no longer stopping to see if any kind voice will address him, and offer him food and shelter. He feels now as if the offer will only madden him, or beat him down utterly, by a relapse into any kind of emotion.

He stops for a while by a smith's forge, the man happening to be engaged in some special

occupation that keeps him late ; and two or three
lads are hanging about the door ; and the stranger
stops by their side, tempted by the glow and
warmth, for he is cold though the time is yet
summer. The smith does not notice him, and
the boys, after exchanging glances among themselves are silent as if in awe ; the man, though
young, looks so haggard and forlorn in all his
mysterious silence.

Presently he goes on again, heedless of the
passing voices that wish him "Good-night!"
He would speak but cannot for the dangerous
choking in his throat when he thinks of *his*
night in connection with the salutation of "good."

A coach passes with its four horses, and he
sees the light of the lamps thrown far in front,
lighting up the grey, weird-looking trees, and
bringing out their anatomy of trunks and branches
with startling vividness. He stands aside to let
it pass, scowling in answer to the looks that he
fancies are fixed upon him from the coach, but
which he cannot see through the glare.

Strange voices of animals or birds haunt him
as he still presses on, and he has ghastly thoughts
of what may happen to him if he should lie down
on these wild hills and be attacked by wandering
beasts and birds of prey. He has heard of a man
who fell from one of the mountain tops on his

route, and was afterwards found torn by wild cats.

Streams of water come gushing and leaping along down the hill-sides, and he pauses by them to slake his consuming thirst, and to wet his feverish brow; and he sits by them for a time, listening to their music and wondering whence they come and whither they go. And then he asks himself whither he is going. And he starts off again with the restlessness of a madman, as if walking alone could soothe the terrible maladies that press upon him.

He feels weary to death; but feels also he could not easily die if he were to lie down and court the grim monarch. He is so young! There is yet so much life in him! He must walk yet many a mile. Hour after hour must he go on, till the end comes. What end? He cares not to ask, and he finds it impossible to answer. He thinks of one fair, beautiful girl, and that thought always has power over him to prevent him once again giving way to the suicide's cowardly solution of life's problem.

"Am I responsible for my own safety?" he asks, looking up towards the stars which are coming out in wonderful brightness. "Have I not worked for bread, begged for bread, and been refused both? Yes, I may, if it were worth while, comfort myself with the thought—this is not my doing, it is my fellow-men's! And much they care !

" Ha! ha! ha !" There was a loud and terrible laugh heard just then by the inmates of a little cottage as they were going to bed; and they lis· tened in awe, and almost with a curdling of blood, when they could hear no more ;—no reply of companions, no signs of any merrymakers going home from the neighbouring fair—nothing to be seen from their bedroom window on the steep hillside but the dim road, the stone walls, the bordering trees, and that single moving bit of blackness, from which surely the laugh must have come.

The man stopped—evidently giddy—put out his hand, felt his way to the wall, and stopped there, leaning his brow against the cold but not hard stones, for they were covered with thick moss.

" My time is come, I think. Let me die, if I am to die, decently. Where? There seems to be a shed in this field, if only I could get in. But I cannot mount the wall. How dizzy I am ! If I could keep that off, I could bear the pain. I must try."

So thinking to himself by slow and painful efforts of his mind, he strove to feel his way along the wall towards some gap or gate that he saw a few yards off. Every instant he felt as though his consciousness might leave him, and he had a horrible fear of suddenly ceasing to be, so far as consciousness was concerned, and then waking to find he had fallen as one that died suddenly, without, like him, finding death's relief.

He got to the opening and saw it was an accidental break that had been made in the wall—perhaps by a cart striking against it—and which had not yet been mended. He could get through it, he fancied, on his hands and knees. He did so, and descended on the other side into a pool of water, which did not frighten him; it rather refreshed him.

He struggled out of the pool as well as he could, and began to ascend the hill: but was so weak, and so afraid of a sudden failure of his brain, that he again instinctively dropped on his knees, and thus crawled slowly towards the shed.

He reached it—got into it—for there was no door — saw some straw in a corner — crawled across the wet earth to it—and then used his last expiring powers of body and mind to get in among the straw, so that it might envelop him, and—he was at peace. A blank, as of death, closed his eyes, and removed from him all pain.

CHAPTER XXII.

GOOD SAMARITANS.

SOME hours after, Reuben was aroused from a strangely sweet sleep, in which he thought Bella Maxfield had come to him with calm, loving eyes, and outstretched hands, and had borne him with her upwards through a series of ineffable glories, until, as he fancied, they were at the very gate of heaven and about to enter, when the vision passed; and he awoke to the consciousness of the gnawing pangs of hunger, to the pains and aches that seemed to have attacked every part of his body, making life itself a prolonged torture, and to the mental clearness of vision that brought back all his dreadful past, and the possibility of a yet more dreadful future. While he thus lay for a few seconds in a state of anguish impossible to describe, he did not know that he had been awakened by a man who was still there watching him in silence. But when he gave vent to a long-drawn sigh of unutterable misery, the

voice suddenly startled him by the exclamation,—

" Hollo! Who are you?"

Reuben turned round; though in so doing he
suffered such excruciating pain that he must
have cried out if he had not checked himself by
a powerful will, and he saw a rather tall man, in
dark grey clothes, with a thin, pale, long face,
looking like a humble farmer, standing there,
and scrutinising him [narrowly. He repeated
his words,—

" Who are you?"

" A man."

" Well, I can see that. But what did you
want here in my shed?"

" Shelter. I was tired, cold, and ill; and being
unable to go any further, I did not stand on
ceremony, but came here."

" But you can't stay here. What do you mean
to do?"

" Don't know."

" When do you mean to go?"

" When you like. But you must turn me
out; I am too ill to move myself."

" What do you want?"

" To die."

" Oh, come; that's all nonsense. Men were
made to live, and especially young fellows like

you. Come, rouse yourself a bit, while I go to the house, which isn't far off. I'll soon be back."

The man went away, and Reuben dropped back upon the straw and shut his eyes, and tried to relapse into the state of comparative bliss from which he had been awakened. He felt he would have given worlds to have prolonged that vision in which he and Bella were together; the world no longer anything to them, and heaven before them, to be theirs evermore.

Yes, if only that dream could come back to him and hold him so fast that he should never wake more to all this wretchedness! He must try. And he did almost succeed in relapsing, at least into forgetfulness, when he was touched, and then he found an arm gliding under his back, and lifting him up with a kind of rough tenderness; and he felt his lips being opened, and brandy being poured, a few drops at a time, down his throat.

This revived him; and in a few minutes he was able to sit up, and then the farmer called out,

"Now, Billy, where's that basin?" and a pretty little child came forward with a basket, in which was suspended, so that it could not upset, a basin with steaming bread and milk.

"Now, eat that, and do it slowly. No, no!

take time. Don't be greedy. I'm not going to run away with the rest, don't you be afraid of that. There, now, shut your mouth, for I don't want you to talk. Time enough to thank me when you've come round."

Reuben ate, and had at first an almost wolfish, desire to dispatch the whole contents of the basin. But he understood the propriety of what had been said, though his mind was strangely confused, and he wondered every now and then why that sweet, earnest, childish face was there, gazing on him with such looks of wonder. The sweetness of the child seemed in some undefined way to be connected with his dream and with Bella ·Maxfield, though how he could not make out.

"Come, I think you feel a bit better now ?"

"Yes," said Reuben, too exhausted still to be capable of any display of vivid emotion, grateful or otherwise. Life, that had been so rudely assaulted and almost driven from his frame, was coming back again to maintain its right, and was in no mood to do anything else—just for a little while.

"Now, sleep for a bit, if ye can, and I'll go to the Union a few miles distant, and bring a cart to fetch you. I'm a guardian myself, and I can promise you you'll be properly cared for. You shall go into the infirmary."

" The Union!" thought Reuben; and he thought he ought to feel indignant and object; but he could not. He knew he was ill—he believed very ill—and he had no right, or indeed wish, to ask a stranger to take him in. "I suppose I have at least a kind of right there!" he said to himself, and went off to sleep, feeling more comfortable for a warm rug the farmer had brought with him and spread over his emaciated frame on its straw bed before he went away.

About noon, the farmer and his wife and little boy, accompanied by a labourer, came to the shed, and found the stranger youth sleeping uneasily, either through physical pain or bad dreams.

He awoke at the first sound of their voices, and was glad to see the rosy, chubby cheeks again opposite to him, and the large, round, staring eyes, and he could not help holding out his hand to the child.

The child looked at him harder than ever—hesitated—looked at his father and mother, who did not at the moment notice the action, then went forward and gave his hand to the wan stranger, who smiled upon him, and drew him forward by that little hand gently till their lips met, and they kissed; and then a great tear, to the child's wonder, began to roll down the hollow cheek.

The child took its little pinafore and tried to wipe away the tear, but Reuben pushed the child aside, while his face grew darker, and he turned to see what the people wanted.

They came to him, lifted him in their arms, and carried him through the open door into the field, and then down the slope towards the very gap in the wall through which he had entered, where a cart was waiting in the road for him.

They put him in the cart, which had a good layer of straw at the bottom, and propped him up as comfortably as they could in a sitting position, and a labourer sat by his side to support him and prevent him from falling if he should again faint.

But the air revived him greatly, and he looked about with a certain renewal of his old animated glance; and the farmer doubled the great rug and put it over him, and tucked the ends well under him, and then said to the labourer,

"Now, John, be careful, I'll go gently;" and they set off, leaving the farmer's wife, who looked on with a certain languid interest, and the little boy, who was now, on his part, crying at the departure of his new friend.

And so they reached the Union—a large but by no means ugly building, and which might even have been prepossessing on account of the fresh beauty of the landscape all around, only that the high walls and small windows seemed intentionally to deny to the inmates any such right of enjoyment. That thought galled Reuben a little ; but, happily for himself, he was too weak even to suffer acutely. And as to pride—God help him ! that had known too many humiliations of late for anything more to move him deeply : so at least at present he thought.

But, if he shivered inly at the fate that took him into a workhouse, he was not able to resist the genial influence of the comfortable infirmary, the kind matron, and the careful and skilful, though pompous, doctor.

And there for nearly a fortnight did our hero stay, slowly but surely regaining strength, but unable to penetrate even in thought into the immediate future. He wondered how long they would thus treat him with so much consideration. He could not tell, and he felt at last a kind of luxury in refusing to think. But he was not long to be left in doubt. The farmer came one day to see him, and the following conversation ensued :—   .

Farmer Pugh—" Well, my man, I am glad to see you looking so hearty again. Now, I need not tell you this is a workhouse, or that I am a guardian. When men would but can't work, the

industrious ratepayers support them ; when they
can, but won't, we make them. I speak, perhaps,
roughly. Don't mind that. I mean no harm
to you or any one else. What do you propose to
do ? "

Reuben—" Anything."

Farmer Pugh—" Well, that's honest. What
have you been ? "

Reuben—"I won't tell you a lie. I would rather
not tell you the truth. I have no character; at
least, no good one. Must I therefore starve?
The world's sick of me, and I of it. I told you
I wanted to die. I was dying when you restored
me to life again."

Farmer Pugh—"I suppose that gives you a sort
of claim upon me ? Oh, don't be proud and impatient. I shan't trouble you much with obliga-
tions. Men don't get much out of me without a
fair return. You seem inclined to be candid. I
like that. I hate shufflers. Suppose you had a
chance of earning a good character ? Don't
humbug yourself or me ; that'll benefit neither
of us. Men of the best character, if poor, have
now-a-days a hard struggle to get on ; you will
have additional difficulties. Measure the ground
well, my man, and then speak."

" Suppose I own that I have often tried, and
failed ? "

"Well, that's to the point; and, if you perceive no material difference in yourself now than
before—if you are too weak to hold fast to a good
resolution when you do make one—why then,
indeed your case is a bad one. But even then,
you see, you won't benefit much by the conces-
sion. At least, I should think not. It's work or
starve here; and I fancy you won't find it very
different in the world generally, only that here
we are obliged to bring matters, you see, to a
more palpable point."

Every word of this seemed to penetrate into
Reuben's very soul. Shame, indignation, desire
to do or say some violent thing or word, at first
almost transported him with passion, but he remembered where he was, how he had come there,
and with these remembrances came the thought
at last,

" He speaks justly, after all."

Presently his head drooped over the table.
Involuntarily he covered his face with one hand,
and plunged the other into his breast to still
and hide his nervous agitation and excitement.
The hand touched something—grasped it—and
there was a thrill sent through his very soul
with the thought of Bella Maxfield. It was
her locket and portrait he had touched, which
remained safe through his distresses, lying

there, where her image lay, close to his heart.

Once more the old superstitiousness of love revived. It was Bella herself who was present; who came to him at this critical moment, as she had come to him at that other one, when Swell Jack was tempting him back to the paths of villany. He would obey the monition. As he had then, at her visible presence, refused the evil course; so now again, at her unseen influence, he would accept the good course. Perhaps, after all, he was not, as he seemed, ever running round and round the vicious and charmed circle that his life seemed to him; perhaps he was, after all, advancing; and if so, whither but to her?"

He began to walk up and down the ward, the farmer watching him in a quiet way but saying nothing, and purposely waiting to hear him speak first.

As he moved he grew more animated, till he seemed to pace quite buoyantly across the floor; and then he turned and suddenly stopped right before the farmer, and said:—

"I thank you! You have done me good. I can now say to you there is a great change in me. I feel and think as I never felt and thought before, when determining upon a new life. I will have more patience; I will bear with greater equanimity what must be borne. Yes; help me! try me!"

"Very good. I shall send you at first upon the road to break stones."

"To break stones!" said Reuben, with a blank aspect and somewhat of a crushed feeling visible even in his very form.

"Yes; that is the only work the parish has for you. That's the field, my man, upon which, as they say in books, you must win your spurs. It is honest labour, depend upon it; and nothing honest degrades a man."

"True; very true," said Reuben, after a deep pause.

It was a somewhat new philosophy to him; but he was in a mood to become a quick scholar. The farmer-guardian went on,

"I shall not lose sight of you. If you make something of yourself there's no saying what may be done for you; but till you have accomplished the one, I shan't be inclined to try the other."

"When may I begin?"

"On Monday morning, if you are strong enough. I will lend you some extra clothing, send you to a sheltered spot, and give orders that your hours of labour be regulated to your strength. No thanks! My maxim is to do my full duty to others, and make others do their full duty to me; and then what room for thanks?"

"Yet I thank you," said Reuben; and the farmer looked at him, and seemed to see a something in his face strangely out of keeping with the talk that had taken place, and with the work that was going to be done, and for a moment his heart smote him, as if he were doing a harsh and unkind act, but it was for a moment only. He put out his hand, and said simply, without another word of comment,

"Good morning!"

Reuben shook it warmly, and they parted; and Reuben sat down to reflect on his labour of Monday.

CHAPTER XXIII.

A DESPAIRING LETTER.

One day, about this time, a letter in a strange hand reached Bella, and fortunately, as she afterwards said to herself, while her mother was busy in the dairy and did not notice the postman's visit. She looked at it before opening with that curious wonder which people so constantly feel who, not being used to receive many letters, find an unknown one come to them. This was addressed in a man's hand—a firm, bold hand it was—but perfectly new to Bella. She opened it with a little misgiving, and found within another letter addressed to herself, the first glance at which brought the blood to her cheeks, and then the tears to her eyes; and then she was obliged to sit down, she felt so shaken physically by the unexpected circumstance.

She put the dear letter into her bosom while she read the open note that accompanied it, which

was addressed from Penmaen, N. Wales, and ran
thus :—

"Madam,—I know nothing about the letter I
herewith forward to you, but there is a something
about the address that suggests that the writer
did not expect it to reach you while he lived.
Let me, then, hasten to inform you that he is
safe. I found him senseless in a shed of mine at
daybreak, and this letter was picked up in the
road, where I fancy he had dropped it. I write
this to you as the only friend or relative of his
of whom I have any knowledge, thinking perhaps some special and family reason may have
driven him from home, and that you may be
glad to know how to find him. For the same
reason I have said nothing to him about the
letter, for he is still low, and it might excite
him, and he might wish to stop me from taking
this step. But, I repeat, he is safe now, and
you need be under no anxiety as to his present
illness.

"I am, Madam, your obedient servant,

"RICHARD PUGH."

Taking the inclosed letter with trembling
fingers she read the address to herself, and then
this startling sentence, written very small, in the

corner :—" If this should fall into any one's hands, the writer begs, in the name of humanity, that it may be forwarded unopened to the person to whom it is addressed."

She hurriedly opened the letter, that must have been written to her under such an awful prospect as that of impending death. It was as follows :—

"On the road to God knows whither.

" Madam,—Though I have no right to address you, even when I know it must be for the last time, perhaps you will forgive me for saying what I am about to say when you know my unhappy state and recollect that the offence will never be repeated.

" I am not about again to afflict you with my story; neither am I about to defend myself as regards my recent efforts, or to attack the world, though it does act hardly by me. No; I want to do very little; but that little is to me everything in this moment of anguish. I want to tell you what I have never dared to tell; what now, I know, will entitle you to inflict any punishment on me, if you do not pity me instead.

" Bella Maxfield, I love you! That is what I want to say. It is the one glory of my life that I loved you the first hour I saw you, that I have never since then hesitated between you and a life of honest industry, on the one hand ; and the loss of you and abandonment to a thousand indulgences and vices in connection with a return to my old career, on the other.

" Yes; I do indeed love you, as men only can love whose nature is driven in upon itself from all directions—finding only enemies everywhere, except with the one, and there it is no longer love but passionate worship.

" I have failed. The world will not have me back. Probably I shall succumb under the struggle soon. If I do, this letter, which I shall keep about me, will, I trust, reach you. If I do not, you will know nothing of this. Farewell, then, for ever ! unless it be that God may be more merciful than man, and I may yet meet you in Heaven.

" REUBEN POLWARTH."

*   *   *   *   *

A few days later, and while Bella remained in a state of ceaseless agitation, wishing to do something, yet seeing nothing that it was right for her to do, Mrs. Maxfield called out one morning as they sat at breakfast,

" Why, dear me, Bella, here's Mrs. Jessop ! "

" So there is," said Bella, with a flush of pleasure as she rose from the table and ran out to the door.

"Well, we have come to see you at last—me and pony!" said Mrs. Jessop.

"And I am so glad to see you, and so will mother be. Come in!"

And the warm-hearted girl took her hand and led her into the parlour, where Mrs. Maxfield also received her very kindly, and they made her sit down and eat a hearty dinner.

Of course they chatted as ladies only can chat, during and after the meal, and nothing was said about the object of the journey. But an hour or two latter, when there was a pause in the supply of topics to be discussed, Mrs. Jessop said, in her demurest tone of voice, as if the matter were of no consequence,

"You had a stranger here a little while back, hadn't you?"

"Yes," said Mrs. Maxfield, who always answered questions put to her daughter that seemed to have the slightest connection with Reuben. "He was a wool buyer, he said."

"He was a London detective!" said Mrs. Jessop.

"A what?" exclaimed Mrs. Maxfield; and the sudden flight of all colour from Bella's face showed her surprise at the news.

"A detective—a man who hunts up rogues and bad people."

"But stay," said Mrs. Maxfield; "let me understand. I know his chararter as a wool-buyer was assumed; he told my daughter so in effect; but he then told her that he came as a friend of—that young person——"

"A friend, indeed! My husband thinks he'll prove the gentleman's worst and most cruel enemy. Some one saw him on the coach, and told my husband so only yesterday."

Why does Bella suddenly remember she "must go up stairs for something" she had forgotten? Why does she not come back? Why has she locked her door, and thrown herself on her bed in an ecstacy of alarm and anguish? Mrs. Jessop knows too well what the disappearance means, and she sees her with the eye of pity very much as she is, and her heart grieves for the poor girl.

Bella reappears at tea time, and looks calm and composed, though there is a redness about the eyes impossible to be concealed.

Mrs. Jessop makes no further allusion to the detective or Reuben, and the two ladies follow her example. She goes off soon after, with a warm request from Mrs. Maxfield that she will come again; but Bella seems to have almost forgotten even the duties of hospitality in the shock she has received from Mrs. Jessop's news, and in the knowledge that, if the detective does overtake Reuben and bring down final ruin upon his head, it is she—miserable girl!—that will have guided him to his prey.

But, is that to be borne? she asks herself as she ascends to her chamber, and locks her door again, and again gives way to a sort of madness of grief. Is it to be borne? *Is she to do nothing?*

A few minutes later, while Mrs. Maxfield was eating a bit of apple-pie and drinking a glass of ale—her favourite supper, when she dared to enjoy herself in spite of indigestion—Bella walked in, erect, stately, pale; but so self-possessed, and with such a strange expression on her face, that the mother knew instantly there was something the matter, and began impatiently to wonder if they ever should get rid of this miserable young man, who haunted their spirits, when he could no longer be present at their hearth.

" I am glad you have come down, dear," said Mrs. Maxfield. " Shall I give you a bit of pie?"

" Mother, you heard what she said?" asked Bella, in a voice that did not sound like her own.

" You mean——" and there Mrs. Maxfield waited for Bella to finish the sentence. But Bella was silent, knowing that her mother knew quite well her meaning. So the former went on,

"You mean about Polwarth?"

"Yes."

"Well, what of it?"

"It was I who told the detective of his letter to us from Chester, whither he has gone to hunt him down."

"Well, dear, you did it innocently enough, you know. Nobody can blame you, whatever happens."

"I shall blame myself."

"Come, come, Bella, this is nonsense. It is, indeed. He's gone away. Do let us forget him."

"I shall never forget him."

"Bella!"

"It is true, mother."

"I am ashamed to hear you say so."

"It is true, mother," Bella repeated, with a tone and manner utterly strange to Mrs. Maxfield.

There was then a long pause. Mrs. Maxfield would have given the world—so she felt—to speak out all her thought on the subject; but she did really love her daughter, and was conscious that she might in one unlucky minute create a discord that might last for a lifetime. Love and prudence alike, therefore, made her cautious.

" Mother," continued Bella, a minute or so later.

" Yes, dear."

" What can be done ? "

" Nothing."

" Something *must* be."

" It cannot, indeed. I wonder you think of it. Would you have me go off to Chester to find him ? A pretty wildgoose chase that would be. Don't be so silly, child."

Bella sighed deeply, and let her head drop into her hands, as she supported them with her elbows on the table, and seemed to forget for awhile all she had been saying. Then she would suddenly close her hands in a hard grip, and press them impatiently against her forehead, as if wrestling with some thought that from time to time agitated her.

"I must do it! I must, mother, if you will not or can not; " she said at last, looking up.

" You ! " said Mrs. Maxfield, in almost speech-less amazement.

" I must warn him, if I can find him, and if there be yet time."

" Bella, I tell you what it is : your wits are fast leaving you. Go to bed—do ! You shall not be guilty of any such abominable absurdity; not while I live, I promise you."

"Mother, I was afraid it would come to this. I have prayed it might not, but I said I could not help it if it did. And it has come. I have never till now disobeyed you. Oh, mother, mother! forgive me—forgive your own daughter when she says she must do this. She cannot sleep in her bed another night and know that the man she has set upon his track may even now be nearing him and plunging him into utter misery and ruin."

As she said this she dropped on her knees to her mother, and the tears streamed down her cheeks; but even as she spoke she was so carried away by her thoughts that she rose again and dashed the moisture from her eyes, and stood as if it was no longer a question about whether she should go, but only how it was to be done and when, for the minutes were precious.

Seeing, however, the state of her mother, who had also risen from her seat and seemed about to give way to a torrent of reproach, she said suddenly, in an altered tone of voice,

"Mother, I scarcely know what I am saying or doing. But listen to me. I love Reuben Polwarth. I shall never love any but he. I have never told.him this in any way. I promise you, before God, I never will tell him without your permission while you live to give it to me, if only you will believe me now—and help me now—to save him, if his salvation be yet possible."

"How could you do this without compromising yourself and me?"

"By simply thinking of my obvious duty—a duty that I should consider I owed to any one in his position who had done for us what he did—even if—I had no individual reason. I would endeavour to find him—give him a single warning word—say why I had done so (that it was I who had unwittingly sent the hunter upon his track), and then, without another word, I promise you that I would leave him and return to you—glad and grateful for the opportunity afforded, even if my heart were to break afterwards."

"Very fine talking! But you could not find him——"

"Let me try."

"And if you did you could not leave him—not —without——"

"Oh! mother, you do not know what a woman who loves can do—even if it is necessary to seem to be against love itself—on occasion."

"And how are you to travel?"

"The carriage will take me, and the man and the boy to the railway. The boy then shall bring the carriage back, while Mattie and I will go on by rail to Chester; and then we will be guided by circumstances—as to whether we proceed by rail or get a pony for me, while Mattie walks, or take a carriage. I have a little money, you know, mother, coming to me when I am of age; I will pay you, out of that, every shilling I expend. I and Mattie will take care where we lodge. You can trust his experience as well as my carefulness."

"Oh, I wash my hands of the whole affair! If you are determined to go, I shall say no more. Only I hope you may not repent it afterwards!"

"Then I may? Oh, dear, dear mother." And Bella's stern resolve now began to melt away in tears, and she threw herself on her mother's breast. Presently, looking up, she said,

"Now, mother dear, listen to me. I know how strange this is; but I will be careful—I will indeed. I will take care to ask no questions myself—do nothing I can help to compromise myself. Mattie shall do all that for me. Believe me, mother, I don't want at some future day to look back upon this one with humiliation and shame. God knows I may be obliged to look back on it with life-long sorrow and disappointment, but not with shame. Be comforted, then. Be at rest about me. You will, won't you?"

But Mrs. Maxfield now began to cry in a feeble, querulous sort of way, and no more was said that night on the subject.

The next morning at breakfast the servant brought Mrs. Maxfield a note, which made the poor mother change colour only to look at unopened. She guessed rightly its purport :—

"Dearest Mother,—Mattie and I are off before daybreak, to spare you the pain of a formal parting. I repeat to you all I said last night—every word of it. You understand? Look for me soon back, with my full promise to you redeemed. Heaven bless and preserve my ever dear, dear mother !

" Bella."

CHAPTER XXIV.

ALL through the Sunday Reuben found it impossible to avoid thinking of the morrow, and the duty it would bring. Should he refuse? Then he must go away at once. More: he must go away in disgrace with the man who had saved his life, and show that, after all, his word was nothing. Had he not pledged himself to Mr. Pugh to submit even to the terrible ordeal of stone-breaking?

But ought he to have exacted such a promise? Could he not see that Reuben ought not to be subjected to such humiliation? But then, the guardian and farmer seemed perfectly insensible to a gentleman's feelings on the point, and able only to say,

"It is honest labour, and it is due to the parish which supports you, and has greatly befriended you."

All through the service at the chapel Reuben

felt rebellious and unable to listen in a proper frame of mind. The same at night; the same when he got up the next morning. Only it is to be noticed that he mechanically got himself ready for the work, and went without a word, under the guidance of an old man who was going on the same business elsewhere, to a spot where two cross-roads met, and where a heap of stone had been thrown down ready for mending the adjacent few yards of each road.

But the stone-heap was in a warm corner, sheltered by a hedge, and canopied by a magnificent oak. The old man showed him how to sit on the little stool, and made him put on the extra coat the farmer had sent from his own house according to promise, and then was about to initiate him in the art and mystery of stone-breaking. But, after a few brief explanations, Reuben cut him short by saying,

"That'll do, thank you:" and the old man went off, though he could not help slily looking back to see if the young fellow was beginning. But the young fellow was not beginning; no, he was savagely and suspiciously eyeing the old man's movements, and evidently determined to do nothing till he was out of sight.

"Well, come," thought Reuben to himself, after leaning a little while on his hammer, hesitating even now whether he should begin or throw his hammer with an oath after the old man and run off—to seek once more his own unaided, unguided way. "Come, hang it, what he says, after all, is right. There is no degradation in this, though there may be a confounded deal of unpleasantness. There!" And, with the word, Reuben let fly with right goodwill, and laughed to see how he had sent a score of pieces flying in all directions.

And then, somehow, there seemed a sense of destructive pleasure to come over him with every blow. He never struck without thinking of something or somebody that he felt inclined to smash; and, over and above all, he felt a kind of vindictive joy in thinking it was Fate herself that he was now hitting so hard, in return for bringing him to such a pass.

Every stone, too, became a sort of embodiment of his past difficulties, and it seemed as though he must be opening some new way as he went right through the heart of the stony mass.

Suddenly, just after striking with all his force at an unlucky stone in this spirit, he heard a laugh. He looked up. It was the farmer, on horseback, who said to him,

"There! You'll have to fetch all those pieces

off the road, you know, before you go away. Mind, my man, it is in breaking stones as in breaking bad habits and most other bad things: one well-directed hit, of sufficient force, is more effective than half-a-dozen vague blows, however tremendous. And then, too, you husband your strength instead of wasting it."

"Ha!" returned Reuben, striking another stone just in the same style, but with still greater violence, "you don't know what good it does me to let fly in earnest. There!" said he, laughing, as he made the farmer guard himself from the rattling shower of small shot that flew about him; "there! I've settled a good many social and philosophical problems in that last blow. No doubt I shall get economical and prudent in the use of my powers by-and-by, particularly if you propose to keep me at this kind of work."

The farmer rode off, laughing, and saying nothing in answer to Reuben's last hint; but Reuben felt that he had pleased his rough friend, and he could not help being himself pleased at the conviction. So he determined to be patient—to pocket his pride—and look upon this stone-heap as his first real step upwards in life.

Let us leave him for a time to the enjoyment of his new philosophy, and look after the detective and Bella Maxfield, who, unknown to the former, were running a race as to which should first reach Reuben.

Bella and her protector Mattie reached Chester without any kind of adventure, and thence went into Wales by the railway going towards Holyhead, which they quitted only when within a few miles of the place mentioned in Farmer Pugh's letter; and where they obtained a light open carriage, which Mattie was to drive.

As she drew nearer and nearer to her journey's end, Bella managed to make herself exceedingly uncomfortable, and to get often very hot in the face by recollecting what an unprecedented kind of thing it was she was undertaking; and by fancying it possible that either Reuben or his aristocratic father might subsequently visit upon her innocent head the scandal that might arise from such a journey. But she never hesitated for a single moment, never confused for a single moment the two different facts—her personal danger and her duty to him. She must go on, and must bear the consequences if any injurious result followed.

She wondered where the detective was—in this the last hour or two, as she hoped, of her outward journey. She gazed anxiously at every man who met them, whether on foot, horseback, or in carriages. She turned to examine every rider whose horse she heard coming on swiftly behind, as if to pass them. She made Mattie walk slowly by every wayside cottage, as if to rest the horse, but really to enable her to give one piercing, rapid glance at the window and into the interior, not only because the detective might be lurking there, but also because she fancied it just possible that Reuben himself might be somewhere in this neighbourhood, and not at the farmer's own house.

She saw at one place a man sleeping on the grass along the roadside, and was so haunted by the idea that it might be the detective who had seen and recognised her as they approached, and had thrown himself down, pretending to be asleep, that she caused Mattie to return and wake him, and ask him the way, while she drew her hood close round her face so that she might not be known. It was a poor old wandering beggar, whose face and voice set at rest in a moment Bella's fears.

Again they went on till they reached and were about to pass an inn—"The Cross Foxes "— where she saw a face just for a moment glance out of an upper window and disappear, as if the tenant of the room were walking to and fro, and had looked out in passing. While the horse had some water given to it to drink, Bella waited in the hope to see the face again ; but it did not show itself ; and even so small a fact as that set the imaginative girl wondering who was in that room and how she could learn.

The hostess came out, and said to her, in a kind, motherly way.

"Won't you come in and rest a bit, Miss?" Bella hesitated, and said,

" Have you no one within ?"

" Only a strange gentleman, who came an hour ago, and seems very tired."

" I must know who that strange gentleman is," thought Bella to herself, and then said to the woman, " Well, if you please to let me just warm myself, for I am cold though the weather is so fine."

" Shall the horse be taken out and have a feed ? "

" No, no; don't move it, keep it there," said Bella, nervously; and then added, in a quieter tone, " I don't want to stop long." Then they went into the house, where Bella took her seat in the fireplace, which was large enough to make a small room, and ornamented with all sorts of bright utensils.

Presently Mattie came in, and was about to take a seat at a respectful distance from his mistress, but Bella whispered to him,

" Don't leave the horse a moment. I'll send out the ale to you."   And Mattie went.

While the woman was getting his ale, Bella listened for the steps above, which she had heard quite plainly when she first came in. But there was no sound. Had he gone? And so instantly on her arrival? Somehow, the thought of this unseen man made her very uncomfortable, even though she remembered the beggar, and how heedlessly she had been alarmed.

" I thought you said there was a strange gentleman," remarked Bella, a little timorously, as though she had no right to comment on such a subject.

" Yes; he's just gone. I thought he was going to stay a bit, for he seemed so tired, and asked me if I could give him a cup of tea with his chop. But he altered his mind, I suppose. That's all."

That might be all to the hostess, but it was or seemed a great deal more to Bella, who was perfectly horrified at the incident, slight as it must have seemed to her under any other circumstances. Had he seen her, guessed her errand, and at once flown off to follow up, before she could interfere, the intelligence he might fancy he had at last got ?

She could not, of course, give any answer, except the practical one to hurry herself and Mattie off, and to watch if they overtook the stranger, and to mind that they did not unconsciously pass him.

She saw a little village in the distance, and could dimly perceive some forms grouped together. "Is he there, inquiring for Reuben?" she wondered, and begged Mattie to urge the horse on, who was tired with a long pull up hill, and weakened with a long season of hard work.

The group were collected about a smith's forge, and the people were boys, with a woman or two, and the smith, with his heavy leather apron. But she saw a form gliding away as they approached, and when they came to the spot the group had dispersed, the smith had gone to his anvil, the form had disappeared.

Did that form belong to the stranger of the inn? She could not tell; but it seemed so natural to her to think so in her present highly-excited state of mind that she forgot to remind herself that she had no proof of any such identity; and if she had, what then? The stranger might have been merely asking his way.

It was now, probably, about three o'clock. Up to this moment there had not been much sun. The sky, though fair on the whole, had been occasionally overcast, and given them fears of rain. But suddenly the sun burst out in fullest splendour and lit up into wondrous beauty the vale through which they were passing, and which might be the same, Bella thought, as that through which Reuben had passed on the last and terrible night which had brought him so nearly to death. The warmth and brightness at once gladdened and relieved her, and she was just saying to Mattie,

"How beautiful! Is it not?" when Mattie caught her wrist with his left hand, and held it in a most significant grasp, without, however, saying a word or making any gesture beyond that of turning his eyes in a particular direction.

Following them, Bella saw, with a thrill of horror, the shadow of their vehicle projected upon the ground, and an odd-shaped something hanging from it underneath that was no part of the vehicle, but looked very like a part of a human being who was clinging there.

She glanced with a pallid face at Mattie, who smiled back a cheery smile, and whispered,

"Shall I spill him suddenly, and stop him from taking any more such liberties?"

"No, no, no!" she replied, in the same low voice. "But we must get rid of him. Perhaps it is only a boy who wants a ride."

"Very likely, Miss."

"He mustn't go any further with us."

"Very well."

"But don't let him think we saw."

"All right, Miss." Then he began in a loud voice to say, "I think, Miss, as soon as we turn this corner of the road, I'll get down and walk a bit, for the horse do seem uncommon tired."

"Yes, if you please," said Bella, trying also to speak loudly yet with unconcern, but feeling herself all over in a tremble.

They rounded the corner, which gave, as Mattie had anticipated, the mysterious personage below them an opportunity to profit by what he had heard, and get away unseen; and, half a minute later, when Mattie also got down, there was no one below the vehicle, nor was there anyone to be seen coming along the road after them.

"Of course not," said Mattie sententiously to himself, and not a little pleased at his own ingenuity in so quietly getting rid of a dreaded companion, who might be a robber, even if he were not the detective.

"Drive fast now, Mattie! Faster! Still faster! Thank you. Oh, no! I am not frightened at the speed. Don't hurt the horse. That will do. He cannot now overtake us."

"Certainly not, unless he has got a pocket edition of the seven-leagued boots to help him," said Mattie, laughing.

On they went for another half-hour or more, keeping the horse to his utmost speed, while Bella looked back from time to time to see if she could obtain any glimpse of the object that had haunted her in so many places, and which now she felt sure was the detective. He must have discovered her somewhere on the road—probably at the inn—have posted on in the hope of antici- pating her; then failing, and seeing her pass, must have resorted to the desperate expedient of going with them unknown to either, and so making them again the instruments of his devilish trade. So she felt and reasoned, and at last accepted it as a fact, though still so little proved, that it was the detective who was behind her.

Yes, thank God, behind her! She was now at all events sure of that. One word might warn Reuben; he might fly—he could not refuse to take their vehicle—her purse—and so he would at once outstrip pursuit.

While her thoughts thus ran away with her, Mattie said to her,

"I see a man breaking stones yonder. Shall we speak to him? We are near the farmer's, and he may direct us."

"Yes, do," said Bella, again looking back, to be sure no one followed. Poor girl! she was soon to perceive that her cares lay before her, and not behind; for, as the vehicle begins to stop, and she looks indifferently towards the man, there is an inward shock, as though she had broken a blood-vessel—she thinks she sees Reuben there.

"Oh, God help me! I am going mad, as my mother said. It is a delusion." But while she speaks the man sees her, and there is no longer any room for doubt—it is her lover—breaking stones by the wayside!

CHAPTER XXV.

"Mr. Polwarth!" exclaimed Bella, startled out of her ordinary reserve and timidity by the sudden spectacle of her lover's occupation.

"Miss Maxfield!" said Reuben, in answer, with almost equal surprise and emotion, though he kept himself sternly under control, and only showed what he felt by the bright red spot that burned on his cheek.

"What means this?" faltered Bella, in a low tone of voice. Reuben rose from his stony throne and came to the side of the vehicle, hammer in hand, while Mattie discreetly made some excuse for going to the horse's head, to put himself out of the way.

"What means it? Oh! simply this. All other vocations are denied me, and I have been persuaded, perhaps foolishly, into thinking even this preferable for a time to the old way of life."

"But you do not mean —— " said Bella, almost passionately; "you cannot mean that, without fault of your own, you have been reduced to this? The world could not be so cruel—so, so wicked!"

"Oh! don't find fault with the world. It's a very good world for the rich, and the comfortable, and the lucky. And if it does bear rather hardly on the poor, and the miserable, and the unfortunate, and the guilty, whose guilt is itself half misfortune, who cares? The poor can do nothing. And that's the only argument—force—now-a-days that anybody listens to."

"Oh, Reuben!—Mr. Polwarth!—don't, don't, I entreat you, give way to this dangerous bitterness of mind. I feel for you; thousands of other people would feel for you and help, if they only knew."

"But then, you see, they take care not to know, except in such gentle ways—in such un-exciting bits of detail—that the knowledge won't hurt them—won't make them enjoy their dinner the less; on the contrary, will rather add a zest to the flavour of the meal."

Seeing her appeal to him neglected, Bella's heart gave way, and the tears fell so fast that she was obliged to turn to hide them; and Reuben saw, and his face seemed to become as dark and lurid as a storm-cloud just before discharging its perilous freight.

"Miss Maxfield, it is quite natural that you and I should see things from a different point of view. You must feel well disposed towards the world, for it has been kind to you—it could not well be otherwise."

Reuben paused a moment as if overmastered by emotion; but presently he resumed in nearly the same tone of voice and manner, as if the interruption had been merely accidental.

"But if you pass through what I have passed through;—but no, I will say nothing about that. I have been guilty, and perhaps am not the best judge of how far my guilt is due to the evil of my own nature or to the influences that poisoned my life at its very outset. No; I will say nothing of myself but that I suffer, and am willing to suffer, if suffering will entitle me once more to the rights of manhood. But I have seen and felt within the last few weeks what I never saw and felt before—how the innocent poor fare in their own land; how they are lodged; how they struggle on; and then how they are treated if inevitable misfortune overtakes them. And yet these are the only people who have been kind to me. Over and over again, my life has almost depended on receiving aid from those who were themselves in the greatest danger of hunger if they lessened unnecessarily their little stores."

"Tell me. I should like to hear of some of these things," said Bella, feeling instinctively the narrative would do her lover good, and enable her to linger yet a few minutes longer with him before she must speak that which she came to say. But even while she thought this she remembered Reuben's danger from her pursuer, and looked back with a shiver of alarm.

Reuben saw and misconceived the look. To him it said that she was reminding herself of the propriety of getting away as soon as possible, although her words were, like herself, kind and considerate.

"It is useless, Miss Maxfield. It would only make you uncomfortable if you believed me ; and I should be sorry if you did not." Then turning away from the subject, he added, abruptly, "Of course, this is some strange accident—our—our meeting ? "

" No, no ! "

"Indeed ! " and Reuben's face grew strangely agitated, in spite of his utmost efforts to remain calm.

" I came to warn you of danger."

" Danger ! and to me ! " said Reuben, with a bitter smile, that expressed in an instant to Bella all his profound despair of soul, and again left her almost unable to speak.

" Yes, a man came to our house—a wool-buyer, he called himself. Mother was not at home. I saw him. He managed to talk about you, and when I grew angry, apologised; and told me a wild story about you and your father, and that he was seeking you for your own good, and I believed him, and gave him your letter from Chester to read. And I was so full of hope for you, till the other day Mrs. Jessop came over to us on a visit from the ' The Traveller's Joy,' and told us that her husband had heard that this man was a London detective —— "

"A detective !" exclaimed Reuben, with startling violence; then remembering himself, he apologised to Bella, and begged her to go on. She noticed, however, that he threw the hammer back on to the heap of stones, and began to prepare himself in all those little but unmistakable ways that show when a man expects to be either immediately attacked, or himself driven to attack.

"Yes; and I found that Mr. Jessop, like myself, had been deceived by his story into helping him to trace you."

"But where is he now ? Do you know anything of his movements," asked Reuben, with quickness, but also with calmness, as though he were mentally recovering all his old activity in times of danger.

"I saw him an hour ago."

"Ha!" exclaimed Reuben, jumping upon the stone heap, and taking a rapid glance over the surrounding country.

"And where?" he asked.

"We passed him, I fancy, two or three times on the road. But at last, fearing to miss us, and thinking perhaps we knew exactly where to find you, he (or some one whom I fancy to have been him) got up behind the carriage, and rode there, and we should have known nothing about it but for the shadow that we saw cast upon the road."

"And did you know where to find me?"

"Yes, of course," said Bella; and was going to add, "your last letter told me." But she remembered suddenly the declaration of love there made, and the colour began to burn in her cheek, and she stopped.

"Forgive me—time is precious. I will not be taken, be assured of that. But it will be best to shun violence, if——"

"Violence? Reuben! Reuben!"

"Tell me; how did you find me?"

"By your letter," said Bella, dropping her eyes.

"My letter? The one I lost. That was not intended to be sent to you, unless ——"

"No, no! I know. Thank God you are safe. Ha! There he is, Reuben! Behind you, crossing the field. Fly!"

"Farewell! Eternal gratitude to you for this. Do not fear; I'm strong again. Farewell!"

Their trembling hands took one clinging parting clasp, and we will not say that there was not something even in that silent mingling of hands that went far to violate Bella's promise to her mother. If so, that was all her sin. She did not in any other way show him what she felt or intended; and he was too manly, even if the time and circumstances had admitted, to seek from her any pledge, or even try how she treated his letter in her heart. Thus they again met, to be again instantly separated.

END OF VOL. II.

BRADBURY AND EVANS, PRINTERS, WHITEFRIARS.

www.ingramcontent.com/pod-product-compliance
Lightning Source LLC
Chambersburg PA
CBHW020927120726
47905CB00008B/2411